The Chronicles of Deer Abbey

The Chronicles of Deer Abbey

Margaret of Shaftesbury

Monica Ferris Presents
Minneapolis, Minnesota

In gratitude this book is dedicated to
Mistress Elli Lutemaker

Table of Contents

Why Deer Abbey?

Because it's funny. But it's also appropriate. The stag is a medieval symbol of piety and religious aspiration; and, because a stag finds safety deep in the forest or on mountains, it is also a symbol of solitude and a life of purity — an excellent choice to represent a small abbey of nuns in a rural setting.

With a largely illiterate populace, symbolism figured strongly in medieval art. Every saint had his or her own special emblem, so while today's tourist must consult his guidebook to see who the statue over the door represents, any medieval person could tell him she is a martyr because of the palm branch she is carrying, and the lamb at her feet means she is St. Agnes.

Plants and animals figure in medieval and Renaissance paintings as personal emblems or to underline or strengthen a point. A freshly-snuffed candle on the table would indicate that the figure in the bed was not asleep, but dead. A painting of a beautiful woman holding a branch of lilies would mean the woman is the Virgin Mary. The painter might further clarify her identity by painting a fountain nearby, by embroidering her dress with strawberries, by planting an almond tree in the background, and by putting the garden in which she sits within a wall.

Deer Abbey's proper name is *Abbatia Cervi Albi*, Abbey of the White Stag. The manner in which he appears (with a shining Cross in his antlers) is from the legend of St. Eustace, who was once Placidus, a rich young Roman hunter, who chased a white stag many miles before it turned suddenly and displayed a shining Crucifix in its antlers, from which experience he was converted to Christianity.

give us this day

From matins to compline at deer abbey

margaret of shaftesbury

1436: The World in Brief

The mummy of Tutankhamen is in its 2,761st year in the Valley of the Kings.

The royal title has been conferred on the first of the later Le Dynasty emperors in Abbam, China.

Murad II, Sultan of the Ottoman Empire, is consolidating his position around Byzantium, probing Constantinople for weaknesses.

Basil II is Grand Duke of Russia. (Ivan the Terrible, first Czar, is 26 years from his title.)

The union of the three Scandinavian countries is breaking apart. A peasant revolt in Sweden brought the title of Regent last year to its organizer, Engelbrecht Engelbrechtson.

Vladislav VI, twelve years old, has been King of Poland for two years.

There is no such country as Germany.

Eugene IV is Pope, elected in 1431 as successor to Martin V, who was the first *sole* claimant to the title since 1378. (From 1378 to 1409 there were two, one in Rome and one in Avignon, and from 1409 to 1415 there were *three*.)

Alfonzo V of Aragon conquered Naples last year.

Charles VII is King of France. Placed on his throne by Joan of Arc, he allowed her to be burned by the English as a heretic in 1431.

James I is King of Scotland. He is a good, strong king, and will be assassinated next year.

Owen Glendower, rebel leader of Wales, has not been seen for twenty-five years.

Henry VI, fourteen, is King of England. He is weak, pious, and a little strange. His mother, the

Dowager Queen Katherine, has been living without benefit of clergy with her Welsh Master of the Wardrobe, and they have three boys and two girls. This year Katherine will be sent to the Abbey of Bermondsey, the children will be turned over to the Abbess of Barking, and the Welshman, Owen Tydr (also spelled Tudor) will escape from prison. Twice. Katherine will die, but Owen and the children will come into King Henry's favor.

It is February 5, 1436, a fine cold night, and a watchman leaves the gatehouse to cross the outer court, the inner courtyard and climb the bell tower steps to the platform from which he can grasp the rope and make Adonai send forth her bronze shout... .

Give Us This Day

For those of us living in the cloister of the Abbey of the White Stag, the day begins at midnight with the ringing of the tower bell, the call to Matins. The nuns in the dorter rise sleepily, the light sleepers gently rousing the slugabeds. All dress quickly in the dark, pulling on fleece-lined soft boots to keep away the chill of stone floors. When I arrive from my private quarters with a lamp, they are ready.

I am Margaret Shaftesbury, Abbess, and these nine nuns and two novices are my little flock. We are a small abbey, but our foundations are royal and ancient. Much was repaired and made new by Queen Eleanor of blessed memory, one of whose Crosses stands a day's journey away at Banbury.

Stone steps, narrow and worn, lead down from the dorter directly into the church. Our little church is actually more a chapel, since outsiders virtually never attend and the nave is almost too small to deserve its name. The Sacrist (with my lamp) leads the way, and I come last.

Most of the light in the church is provided by cressets, blocks of stone whose tops are hollows filled with oil, each containing several floating wicks. The altar, of course, has two large candles of pure beeswax. It is very cold and the darkness seems nearly to devour the frail lights. There is a mixed smell of smoke, oil, wax, incense, and, faintly, humanity.

A quick sound of shuffling feet from the rear signals the arrival of Father Hugh Paddington, late as usual. He is a small, brown fellow with kind, anxious eyes, who means well. He stops behind our lectern — a beautiful gilt one, shaped like a pelican slashing her breast to feed her young, her wings outspread to support the Breviary. It is open to the correct page (today is Monday, February 5, the Feast of St. Agatha) but he turns several pages before he realizes that and starts back. He pauses to direct a hard stare at Kat, one of the novices, who turns a giggle into a cough quickly.

The choir where we are sitting consists of two double rows of pews facing each other across a broad aisle. The backs of the rear-most pews rise near twice the height of a man and are richly carved with scenes from the Parables.

Sister Mary has fallen asleep. That's the second time in four days; she shall have no wine for a month. I lift my chin at Sister Elizabeth to get her attention and nod towards the dozer. She leans over and pokes her.

"The Lord is King of virgins; come let us adore Him." Father Hugh has a beautiful light clear voice.

Matins is a long service; every seven days we recite 145 psalms, in addition to other prayers and prayers special to the day. "I am the handmaid of Christ, and for that reason I bear the appearance of a slave." (I really must remove the fur trim from my garb.)

"Agatha went to prison with great joy and pride, like a guest going to a banquet..." (I would rage like a lioness, I am afraid, or weep piteously.) "... buffeted and tortured on the rack with hot plates ... " (Oh dear, I don't like hearing about martyr saints in such gruesome detail in the middle of the night!)

Matins is ended with a Te Deum and followed immediately by Lauds. "O God, who amongst other marvels of Thy power hast given even to weak women the triumph of martyrdom ..." (Weak women and weaker men, I dare say.) "... in the unity of the Holy Spirit, now and forever. Amen."

Now for a small cup of hot spiced wine and back to bed. Thank God for lay cooks, heating things up while we pray.

And up betimes at dawn for Prime. The church is filling with a soft, cold light, and the beautiful stag carved into the front of the altar can be seen as more than a collection of odd shadows. The gold cross caught in his antlers seems to gleam with a light of its own, very pretty. We sing, "Now daybreak floods the earth with light; we lift our hearts to God ... "

After Prime we wash and put on our daytime clothing. My underdress is of very soft and fine wool, taken from our own sheep, washed, carded, spun, woven and dyed black here at Deer Abbey. The outer robe, also black, is of a coarser weave for warmth. My wimple is white, my veil black. I have an ordinary black leather belt (but it has a pearl in the buckle) from which I hang my bunch of keys and my carved ivory rosary. My ladies use white rope for belts and have black rosaries; otherwise we dress alike.

The good smells of baking bread drift through the cloister. Fr. Hugh is available for hearing Confessions. The clamor of the little bell hanging outside the frater door summons us to breakfast: Buttered eggs over warm herbed bread, and a cup of fresh ale. There is barely time to rinse the crumbs from our fingers — we *do* loiter at breakfast, even if it *is* in silence — before Adonai's bronze voice summons us to Chapter Mass (so called because it precedes Chapter).

There are many servants and lay folk attached to the abbey, but they have a quick Mass said by Fr. Hugh while we break fast. Our Mass is a sung one, and we sing in Plainsong the Introit and Kyrie while Fr. Hugh says his prayers at the foot of the altar. He is vested in silk the color of blood in honor of the martyr saint whose day it is; his back is marked with a black velvet cross; and he is no longer a ridiculous little monk but an alarmingly powerful Priest. When he lifts the Host he has consecrated, none dare lift their eyes. It is a fearsome thing to fall into the hands of the living God; not until Easter will any of us take Communion.

The sun is shining brightly through the two tall windows at the east end of the church. In the center, high over the altar, is a cinquefoil window of clearest blue, with a white dove shining in its center. It seems to hover deliberately, to hear Fr. Hugh chant the floating lines of the Lord's Prayer " ... and lead us not into temptation," he sings, and pauses. "But deliver us from evil," we respond and together add, "Amen." Terce immediately follows Mass; we stay in our places for it. "God dwells within her and she stands unmoved." I am often moved by pity or expediency. It is hard to find a workable level of strictness for ladies who need discipline yet because of gentle birth must be handled diplomatically. "O Lord, make haste to help me."

We go in a body to Chapter. Our Chapter House is small. Its walls seem to be mostly colored glass, in the newest style. I have a proper chair to sit in, and I let my crozier rest against my shoulder as my ladies take their places on their backless stools and wait for Fr. Hugh to remove his vestments[i] and join us. It does not take long.

He opens Chapter with a prayer to the Holy Spirit and a reading from the Holy Rule of St. Benedict. We go through the entire Rule bit by bit, and then begin again. It is possible I know it by heart; I have been hearing it since I was a weanling. "Idleness is the enemy of the soul," begins Fr. Hugh. We are into the part about manual labor. I wonder if he was thinking of us when St. Benedict wrote, "But let all things be done in moderation for the sake of the faint-hearted." I recall last harvest time when I agreed with Sister Martha that it might be good for us to help with the harvest. The gathering of sheaves went well, and we picked apples and raked hay to such good effect that we will continue the practice. But when they dragged in the first squealing pig to the slaughtering pen, and the blood shot from its throat onto the gowns of Sisters Martha, Ann, and myself, we became faint-hearted indeed, and withdrew!

But I digress. Fr. Hugh finishes his reading, blesses us and goes to his breakfast in the kitchen. He is a humble priest; he could be served in state in his own little house in the inner courtyard that he shares with his deacon, but prefers to cause less trouble this way.

Next in order is discipline. I state that with my own eyes I saw Sister Mary asleep at Matins this morning, and that Thursday she was sleeping and warned about it. Sister Mary rises and confesses her fault in a high breathless voice, and kneels for her punishment. She is slender and supple, small as a swan's neck, and as white. I nearly retract the punishment I decided on when I saw her asleep, but recall St. Agatha and stand (sit, rather) unmoved. She accepts the punishment of no wine for a month so unflinchingly that I am emboldened not to smile at her when she rises and looks at me.

No one else wishes to accuse or confess anything, so we open the business part of Chapter. Sister Elizabeth, our Precentor[ii] and a tall lady who looks to be made of twigs and parchment, speaks first in her dry voice. "Our copy of *The Bestiary* came back from Sir Richard yesterday with a damaged cover." She is quite upset over it, but since we do not lend out any of our books without holding a borrower's book hostage, we have *The Forme of Cury* from Sir Richard's library, which will not go back until he has *The Bestiary* repaired. Sister Elizabeth suggests that perhaps we could copy some recipes from Sir Richard's cookbook. That is an excellent suggestion, and it will be done.

Our shy Sacrist, Sister Veronica, complains with a nervous flutter of long, immaculate fingers, that Fr. Hugh on Sunday stepped on the hem of his best alb and tore it in such a way that it cannot be invisibly mended. The second-best alb is really not fit for Sunday wear. Work on the new white chasuble goes slowly. If a new alb must be made as well, they may not be ready by Easter — Sister Veronica rolls big frightened blue eyes at me. I refuse to allow anyone to sit up late, burning precious oil and still-more-precious candles. I suggest that a little less talk and laughter during embroidery sessions would see the chasuble quite ready for Easter morning. Lent begins the last day of this month, so Easter is not until April 8, which is plenty of time. I will help with the embroidery on the alb.

Sturdy Sister Martha, our Cellarer, reports we may have a new Steward at last. We have had none since Robin Banbury was carried off by the outbreak of Black Death last Feast of St. Francis (October 4) that also robbed us of Sisters Alys and Joan. John Freemantle spoke to Fr. Hugh about the position when he was visiting the sick in Deerfield a few days ago, and an appointment was made with Sister Martha to interview him. John's family has owned land in this area for many generations. John's father tried to increase the family's fortunes and raise his son a gentleman, but overreached himself. The land was sold to pay his father's debts, and so John comes to us. John knows the ways of domestic animals, especially sheep, and also of grain. We would be lucky to have him, concludes Sister Martha, and he is available now for an interview. God be praised!

Dauntingly tall Sister Katherine, Fraterer, reports that a kitchen scullion was sieving the fine white sand we use to wash our eating knives in the lavatory when she knocked our small whetstone off the shelf. It is in three pieces, useless. She, Fr. Hugh and Simple Jack (our odd-job man) will visit the blacksmith in Deerfield village after Sext to purchase a replacement. As the road is frozen hard, they will walk. — it is not an hour's journey afoot to the village.

Like an empress giving an order, Sister Katherine adds, "Linen change tomorrow!" I catch her eye and frown and she continues, less imperiously, "Leave soiled bed linen by the top of the dorter steps before Prime." She has a high stomach, but is easily intimidated.

I am Farmerer, but none of my ladies are sick, thank God, and it is not yet time to be brewing the spring tonic or for blood to be let, so I have no report to make.

Sister Mary, our Bailiff, reports in her dove's voice that all rents are up to date at last, except from Master Adam, who has owed seven pence since Christmas, and will owe seven more at the Feast of the Annunciation (March 25) although he has paid the eggs and ducks and fish. If after I interview John Freemantle he appears capable, I will send him to Master Adam.

Sister Mary also reports that the cook is asking an extra penny a week. We will see how she handles the difficult Lenten regimen and the Easter feast before deciding.

Sister Mary is a very good Bailiff; our books are neat and are always in perfect order. A pity she cannot stay awake at Matins. Fr. Hugh has not yet returned, and the ladies exchange a word or two among themselves in a whisper. I do not enforce the Rule of Silence as strictly as I ought. I have been Abbess not quite two years, and at first followed the old custom of allowing only the little passageway between the warming room and Chapter House to be used, for urgent conversations. But when I enforce strict silence, my ladies resort to a peculiar method of hand signals current in most abbeys. Signs create more uproar and unseemly laughter than a quick, softly-whispered question or two, and in allowing occasional use of the latter I have forbidden the former.

Fr. Hugh dashes into the Chapter House and begs my pardon for his tardiness. There is a smear of egg on one of his eyebrows. I grant it, but coolly — really, the fellow is at times very tiresome!

Fr. Hugh is our Almoner. We have two people in our Almonry, a dying old lady from Deerfield and a beggarman found Friday at Prime at our gatehouse door. The lady has a sickness that causes her belly to grow as if she were pregnant, and as it waxes she wanes, until she dies of it, probably tonight or tomorrow. Fr. Hugh gives her some of my elixir of poppy to let her sleep. He will give her Last Rites after Chapter. Sister Veronica will go with him and Deacon Piers. The beggarman was beaten by no one knows whom, save the beggarman, and he cannot tell, being deaf and dumb. His lungs rattle, but he may not die. With Chapter over at last — an unusually long one — my ladies go to take out what they will need for their work later on, and I retire to my quarters to await John Freemantle.

My "quarters" consist of one large room whose rear part is separated from the rest by a tall, carved screen behind which crouches my narrow bed and a big chest, which came with me to Deer Abbey and served for a while as my cradle. Four tall windows light well the rest of the room and add splashes of color. The windows hold representations of the arms of Deer Abbey, of Queen Eleanor, and of several former abbesses.

My servant Eulie is poking up the fire, but stops when I enter to take my cloak and crozier. (Her name is Eulalia, a name I care not to pronounce; she was a gift from my mother when I was twelve.) Since I have a fireplace I can indulge a fancy to have only sweet rushes, thinly spread over my blue-and-white tiled floor. Eulie returns to continue tending the fire and I tell her John Freemantle will be here soon. She is tiny, with a twisted back. "Ye'm," she mumbles, shortly. She glances up at me, black eyes glittering through strands of graying hair. "He be good for us. You like him." It was a command.

"I will make every effort," I promise. I go to the fine large table beneath the windows and fit my spectacles to my nose, hooking the loops behind my ears. While I wait for our prospective Steward I may as well try again to translate this old deed (I am doing a history of Deer Abbey). It is a relief to put it down when I hear the bell outside the cloister door sound in warning and then the scrape of heavy wood on stone as Sister Martha brings Freemantle into the little passageway outside my door.

He is a rough-looking specimen, despite his fashionable "bastard" (calf-length) houppeland split fore and aft for riding. I stand as Martha brings him into the room and introduces us. She leaves, to stand outside my not-quite-closed door. (Thus do we still make a small bow towards doing everything communally and not privately to do anything.)

"So, John Freemantle, you are willing to become our Steward?" His coxcomb hat has fallen apart in his hands, and he pulls the liripipe through his work-marred fingers. Earlier he had given an excellent imitation of a noble's bow. Almost gentle, he is like the bat, neither flesh nor fowl. "Ma'dame, I would."

"We have been without a steward for some little while, and things are out of order. The grain we send out does not all seem to come back in flour. Paul the orphan, who was Robin's assistant and whom you have undoubtedly met, has been attempting to straighten the miller out, but he is only fourteen. And our Bailiff may be getting into trouble collecting rents; I would like you to go with her to see one Master Adam. Also, we slaughtered too few animals last November and have not enough hay to last until Spring." I pause. Am I alarming him?

"An it please you, Ma'dame," he begins carefully, shifting his weight so his over-the-knee boots creak. "Perhaps you would allow me to spend a se'ennight going over the land and the accounts. Then I could come back to you better able to say if and how I could put the abbey back into good order."

Glory be to the Father, Son and Holy Spirit for ever and ever! I cannot hold back a smile. "Yes, my son; that is most pleasant and worthy advice. Do not neglect speaking to Father Hugh. He sometimes proves an unexpected source of good information."

"Yes, Ma'dame. Thank you, Ma'dame." And with another creditably-executed bow, he leaves the room. I believe he is something over five-and-twenty, and, though quite tall, he is not at all comely. I shall speak with Sister Martha and Fr. Hugh in two or three days, to see what they think of him.

A sudden clamor wakes me from a pleasant reverie about docile tenants and flour in full measure. Simple Jack is hammering away at our clapperless bell by the frater door, signaling time to wash for dinner. I do wish it were not customary for the bell to ring continuously until everyone is in the frater ready to begin. The ceaseless noise sometimes puts me quite out of temper; even poor Jack's ecstatic gap-tooth grin cannot restore me.

About the time I was born (on the Feast of the Assumption in the year our Lord King Richard Second died, August 15, 1400), the frater was split lengthways along its line of supporting pillars. The western half remained the frater, and the eastern became a misericord. It was at first directed that the misericord was for the use of the sick, the old and the very young, where they were served richer food than the regular fare. But it has since developed that no one uses the frater, and we all eat better than we should. But during Lent, we all eat as of old in the frater.

There is a large painting on the wall of the frater of the Crucifixion, and in the misericord of Jesus in glory. I bow to each on my way to my chair, and those following me in bow to each and again to me. One thing that awful clanging of the bell has done is to bring all of us promptly to our places so I can signal to a novice to run quickly out and make him stop.

We chant Grace ("Bless us, O Lord, and these Thy gifts ...") I hear the shuffle of booted feet on stone as Sister Lucy climbs to the pulpitum built into the far wall. Silence. I lift the small brass bell on the table before me and let it ring once. Everyone sits. It rings again. The careful voice of Sister Lucy floats above our heads. We have been reading Venerable Bede's *History of the English Church and People*. We listen to the first sentence motionless. "Pope Honorius also wrote to the Scots whom he learned to be in error about the observance of Easter, as I mentioned earlier." I ring my bell a third time and my ladies open their napkins, within which each finds a small loaf of bread.

Sisters Martha and Mary are taking their turn this week to sit at my table, and Sister Agnes (last week's reader) is this week's server. She goes to the kitchen and brings the first dish to me, a Brie cheese tart, and goes back for the second, rabbit in wine syrup. She serves us with a very pretty grace, and I sign for her to sit at the foot of my table and begin her own meal.

"In this letter he particularly warned them to beware of and suppress the heresy of Pelagius, which, he learned, was reviving among them." (Why must some continually meddle with the True Faith, twist some part of it back-end-frontwards, or call some part of it a lie? And why do they insist they are Christians? They should call themselves by their true name: heretics! This Brie tart is very nice!)

Empty plates are taken away and the second remove arrives: Parsnip fritters, mutton roasted with camelyn sauce, and a fresh pitcher of ale.

I have eaten many times away from the abbey, in a setting where talk and laughter go on amid the sounds of gnawing and calls for more wine, which can be very pleasant. But back in the silence of our misericord I sometimes feel when dining and conversation are mixed, both suffer.

Those who want the rest of their bread with the evening collation wrap it in their napkins. The remaining bread and the broken meats will be collected and taken by Fr. Hugh to the main gate to be distributed to the unruly lot of beggars who gather there daily.

I ring my brass bell and Sister Lucy looks for, and finds, a natural place to stop. We have not made great progress in the reading, as the reader speaks slowly, and repeats any passage that seems of particular significance. "... in accordance with the Apostle's promise, when he said: 'And if you err in any matter, God Himself will enlighten you.' But I shall speak of this more fully in its proper place." She follows this with the usual, "*Tu autem, Domine, miserere nobis.*"

To which we respond, "*Deo gratias,*" and rise to chant Grace. And immediately begin to chant responsively the 51st Psalm, forming a double file to march to the church for Sext. It is nearly twelve of the clock. "Make me a clean heart, O God, and renew a right spirit within me."

Last All Hallows Eve I told my ladies the story of Titivillus, the devil who skulks about abbeys and monasteries with a big black sack into which he stuffs dropped syllables and stepped-on phrases of monks and nuns in too-great haste to finish their offices. Sisters Elizabeth and Veronica turned up their narrow, well-bred noses at this unsophisticated tale of a devil who gets beaten by Satan if he does not fill three bags full a day. But all the same I have noticed the ladies across the aisle are not so eager to begin their verse of a psalm that they virtually interrupt the ladies on my side. A silly story with a sharp image is sometimes better than a lecture. We chant three psalms amid the brief prayers, and find the morning, with its emphasis on praying, is over, and we have before us the afternoon, with its emphasis on work.

In the winter, our "manual labor" consists mostly of sweeping, dusting and putting to rights our little church — except the Sanctuary, of course; Fr. Hugh and Piers, his deacon, have exclusive charge of that sacred place. We pour more oil into the cressets, fluff up the straw on the floor around the pews, and dust the marble effigy of Sir Edward de Cynegil, who was Sir Richard's father, and Sister Mary's grandfather. His is the only effigy and tomb in our church, although several abbesses are buried near the altar. Sir Edward fought with King Richard against King Henry IV (as he became), and he did not want burial in a place so public as to draw attention to the family's fortune. The de Cynegils were patrons and protectors of Deer Abbey for many generations and continue so today, a necessary article in these lawless times.

But it is a small church and despite the slowness and fussiness of my ladies, the work is soon finished.

Then we separate to perform individual or small-group tasks. Sister Ann, our Novice Mistress, takes Kat and young Harley to the southeastern corner of the cloister[iii] to drill them in the psalms, which they have nearly memorized. The north walk, being warmest, is where those who are doing copy work or embroidery gather. Our cloister walk was once a roofed series of arches around a grassy square. But for more than a hundred years it has been glassed in. Stones now mossy with age filled in between the arches to waist height, and above that to the roof was set colored glass, each arch devoted to a different distaff saint: The Virgin, our own St. Eadburga, St. Hilda, and others.

The sun coaxes warm yellows from the stones of the cloister and lays bright splashes of color around a pillar here, on a table there; and the bright, eager voices of our novices mingle with the chatter of our servants at work, making the abbey seem to be the beehive it is supposed to resemble, a thought which cheers me as I retreat to my quarters to compose a letter to Sir Richard explaining why we are not returning his copy of A Forme of Cury just yet.

My problem is to let Sir Richard know the book left here in perfect order and returned damaged without even subtly hinting that he personally despoiled it.

I am nearly through with my draft when I hear footsteps and voices outside my door in the passageway to the gate that opens into the inner courtyard. A moment later the heavy wooden door groans on its old hinges and Simple Jack, Sister Katherine and Fr. Hugh leave the cloister. I noted the thump and drag of Fr. Hugh's enormous "pilgrim's staff" (a quarter stave if ever I saw one!); I trust he has remembered to take the bread and broken meats with him to the main gate across the outer court. The beggars get very indignant and noisy if they are neglected.

My rough draft completed, I walk around the cloister to see how everyone is getting on. Sisters Elizabeth, Veronica and Lucy have cut the white linen cloth and are fitting Fr. Hugh's new alb together. Sisters Agnes and Cecilia are working with gold thread to embroider his new chasuble.

Sister Martha says she did happen to notice Fr. Hugh coming out of the kitchen with a large bundle apparently containing food. She is copying out recipes from A Forme of Cury in her exquisite Italian hand. I suggest to her that she save some of the work to show the novices how to copy quickly, clearly and beautifully.

On my way back to my room I stop to congratulate Sister Ann on the progress she is making with two promising novices, who blush and drop clumsy curtsies. They are twelve and fourteen years old.

I find on my return the cloister cat Dinah making herself cozy on the stool nearest the fire. It is not until I am some way into my smooth copy of Sir Richard's letter that I realize she has brought a mouse with her and is making it smart for its grain-thieving ways. She misinterprets my interest for covetousness, quickly kills the creature, and proceeds to devour it.

Every color that every cat has ever been goes into the swirl of Dinah's coat, and she has a white chin. She hunts mice and I praise God, and each of us is content.

I finish my letter, not without pain and effort, and fold, seal and address it. Now I have a little leisure time and seek to divert myself with my book of poems. I sit on a stool beside Dinah and warm my toes as I read. The book opens in my hands to a favorite:

> I have set my heart so high,
> I like no love that lower is;
> And all the pains that I may draw,
> I think they do me good, surely.
> For on that Lord that loved us all
> So heartily have I set my thought,
> It is my joy on Him to call.
> For love I have been brought to pain;
> I think it does me good, surely.

I read "I sing of a maiden that is Matchless," and Fr. John Awdelay's "Timor Mortis Conturbat Me," wherein he laments his blindness. A five-line verse on a secular subject I have for prudence placed in this collection of religious and moral poetry, and I turn to it now:

> Since law for willfulness begins to slacken
> And falsehood for prudence is taken,
> Robbing and revenge hold purchase,
> And in vices men take solace,
> England may sing, Alas, alas!

Footsteps and the ring of merry voices signal the return of my wanderers. I open my door to greet them, and they cluster around, brimful of gossip.

It seems that Eleanor Islip, to whom we offered to sell a corrody four years ago over the objections of our Steward, took her silver instead to Godstow. Now she is retiring there, to live in comfort the rest of her days, per the terms of the corrody. And she is taking with her three servants, two horses, four small dogs, a greyhound, a parrot and a monkey! Cecilia Edgehill held a corrody of us, but she took a chill and died right after New Year's Day. Those three are laughing at Godstow, but my knees are weak — it could have been us, by St. Loy! St. Scholastica aid my sister Abbess of Godstow!

They barely have time to rinse the travel stains from their hands and faces before the bell rings out for None.

We are nearly to the end of the first of the three psalms before we are our old selves again, back into the habit of prayer. "I will praise the Lord, as long as I have breath to praise Him ..."

Then back to our tasks for as long as the light lasts. I select a pattern of grape leaves Sister Katherine will trace onto the alb, and we will embroider it. The cook comes humbly into the cloister to pick up those recipes Sister Martha has completed copying and expresses herself pleased with them. Sister Veronica, bent over the pattern she is working in gold thread in the new chasuble, begins to hum a melody that is quickly picked up by the others in song: "I have a young sister far beyond the sea; many be the love-tokens she sent me. She sent me a cherry without any stone, and also a dove without any bone . ." It's a riddle song, rather clever. We sing others, and then, as the light begins to fade and chill sets in, the mood shifts, and someone begins to sing the eerie lines, "Suddenly afraid, half waking, half sleeping, and greatly dismayed, a woman sat weeping ..."

With stiffened fingers and aching toes we retreat to the warming room where a lamp has been lit and the fire built up. There is little conversation; we are subdued by cold, the desire for warm food, and the thought of prayers to come.

The voice of Simple Jack mumbling fragments of a Pater and complaining of cold echoes faintly around the cloister as he shambles toward the kitchen, seeking his supper and a place to sleep. Poor old creature, he is as harmless among the cook's helpers as a gelding among mares, having neither want nor ability in that direction.

Soon Adonai speaks and we enter our church for Vespers. It is cruelly cold, and a rising wind outside sends thin columns in through crevices, making the tiny flames in the cressets flicker. I pull my sleeves over my hands and keep my feet tucked up under my robe and concentrate on the verses of the psalms. Soon I am rapt in the familiar words and feel at ease by the time we begin the Magnificat, "My soul doth magnify the Lord." From across the wide aisle a small cluster of white faces swimming in blackness replies, "My spirit has found joy in God ... "

In silence we hasten to the misericord for supper. Sister Lucy is privileged as reader to miss Vespers so she may eat before us and read to us over our little meal of chicken blancmange with a pittance of cheese and apples. She is reading the part about how King Oswald gave his supper away to beggars, and the silver dish it was served on as well. Bishop Aidan held up Oswald's generous right hand and said, "May this hand never perish." His wish was heard; according to Bede Oswald's preserved right hand and arm are at Bamburgh.

We adjourn quickly to the warming room where around a blazing fire we listen to Sister Elizabeth read from *Piers Ploughman* by the light of the only lamp. "He looked at me keenly and answered, 'Jesus, out of chivalry, will joust in Piers' coat of arms, and will wear his helmet and mail, Human Nature; he will ride in Piers' doublet, that no one here may know him as Almighty God... '"

We have about an hour of reading and discussion, then the bell rings as a signal for Compline. Langland is set aside and my ladies look to me to lead them in the prayers. For Compline we need not brave the cold of the church. The prayers are brief, ending, "The Lord Almighty grant us a quiet night and a perfect end. Amen."

The cook and a helper arrive with a pitcher of hot spiced wine, our cups and leftover bread from dinner for those who saved it. With that sweet warmth bubbling away inside us, it is easy to face the chilly cloister walk.

Eulie is waiting. The fire is freshly banked, she waits with a single candle to light me to bed. "Get out my fur-lined cloak for Matins, please, Eulie," I ask, and she does, laying it beside the soft boots, then helps me off with my outer gown and lays it beside the cloak.

Then she kneels and asks my blessing, and I place my hand on her forehead — this is not something I have any clerical power to do, but she claims it wards off nightmares — and I ask the Lord God to defend her from all dangers and mischiefs, and from the fear of them, that she may enjoy such refreshing sleep as may fit her for the duties of the coming day. "Amen," she says, content.

The abbess who installed my fireplace also covered the exposed beams of the roof with level planks, and made a storage loft thereby, and also made the room easier to heat. Eulie scrambles up a rickety ladder to the loft and tosses down her straw pallet on which she will sleep before the fire. I hear her punching it into a comfortable shape and grunting as she lays down on it. "Matthew, Mark and Luke and John, bless the bed that I lie on," she murmurs, and almost immediately begins to snore.

It takes me a while to drift off to sleep. I go over my tasks for tomorrow (find someone to take Sir Richard's letter to him, begin to embroider the alb, find out what the cook requires for Lent); and wonder if John Freemantle's surname was not, in his grandfather's time, Freeman; and pray that all fires are properly banked and we are not burnt in our beds this night.

As soon as the leaves are the size of a mouse's ear. I will leave on pilgrimage to Canterbury, to see again the tomb of the Holy Blissful Martyr Saint Thomas Becket. I wonder if we'll tell stories on the way, like last time ...

OUR DAILY BREAD

Property, income and policy at Deer Abbey

margaret of shaftesbury

1454: The World in Brief

Christopher Columbus, Ferdinand of Aragon, Savonarola, and Leonardo da Vinci are all about three years old.

Mayapan in Central America was destroyed last year, marking the beginning of the decline of the great Maya civilization.

Constantinople was taken by Mehmed II last year, who made it the capitol of his Ottoman Empire. Today Turks call it Istanbul. Greeks still prefer Constantinople.

Feudal anarchy rose to its peak in Castile.

Cosimo, founder of the Medici family, worked to create a triple alliance of Florence, Milan and Naples.

Nicholas V is Pope. He began the Vatican Library.

Lorenzo Valle recently demolished the *Donation of Constantine* as a forgery.

France had killed John Talbot and driven the English out of Normandy and Guienne.

In Scotland, only Berwick remains in English hands.

Richard, Duke of York, was Viceroy of Ireland. He was very popular there, having brought a measure of independence from England to that unhappy country, including its own coinage. But the Duke was home in England in the spring, putting down some unrest involving the Duke of Exeter — and serving as regent during the King's incapacitation.

England was suffering because of its weak, prudish and sometimes insane King Henry VI. His wife, Margaret, had a son in October of 1453, but he didn't know it yet, having been frightened into a state of catatonia in August. Henry's party at court hated the Duke of York, especially when he became regent. (In 1450 there was a serious rising of peasants, merchants and small land-owners because the popular Duke of York — then heir to the throne — was denied a place on the King's Council.)

It was the first Monday after Pentecost (Whitsun), June 1, 1454. All over England the sheep were gathering to be relieved of their wool. The Chancellor of the Exchequer sat in the House of Lords on a woolsack, acknowledgment that England's economy had for centuries been based on sheep that produce the finest wool in the known world.

Our Daily Bread

"Two fat oxen, three lean country steers under two years of age, ten lean working oxen, seven cows and heifers, three calves, one old bay, one dun, one black and one ambling gray, all mares," intoned John Freemantle, as I wrote.

"Why are we keeping *two* fat oxen?" asked our Bailiff, young Sister Harley, under the prompting of her whey-faced assistant, Edward of Oxford.

"One for us after midsummer and one to feast the workers on at Harvest Home," I replied, and remembered a time when we had so little land and few workers that a pig or even a few geese would have made the feast. Back then we would not have needed to spend all of a lovely spring day taking a count of our income and expenses.

Freemantle shuffled his not-too-clean scraps of paper and continued.

"A white mule, four geldings for the plow, sixteen hogs of diverse sorts, and four suckling piglets."[iv]

"Only four?" I queried.

"She overlaid another last night, Madame."

"She makes a very careless mother," noted stout Sister Martha disapprovingly. She is our Cellarer and takes a personal interest in all our animals.

"If she does not improve, we'll see how much bacon she'll make come St. Martin's Day!" Economics make me cross. "Come, Master Freemantle, count our sheep for us." A lark sang outside the window and a carefree breeze brought the scent of new grass and tender–petaled flowers.

And the sound of sheep. They had arrived that morning to be sheared, our desmane sheep and the sheep from our manor of South Broughton and sheep belonging to our villeins,[v] until the meadow was full of them, freshly washed and newly blessed by Father Hugh. The lambs were being separated from the sheep and the shearers had arrived. The weather looked to be warm and sunny for several days — perfect shearing weather.

"Yester-eve we had 420 ewes and rams and exactly 100 lambs," said Master Freemantle (who is our steward in title and our seneschal in fact).

I sighed after the lark and dipped my pen. "That seems a low number of lambs. Murrain?"

"Three more dead yesterday. We have lost a dozen lambs since Easter, and 27 ewes and rams." And this is only the day after Whitsun! The murrain is the Black Death of sheep; they begin to rot while still grazing. But despite disease we have 50 more ewes and rams than last year; 137 more than the year before. And these are Cotswold sheep, producers of the best English wool, the best in the world.[vi]

It seemed on that bright spring afternoon that all the world went merry but us: we had to sit sealed up in my quarters, counting our possessions and estimating our expenses.

Our cropland has to be marled after this next harvest after a lapse of twelve years. We had increased fertility by ordering that only enough stubble to repair thatch be taken from our fields and the rest plowed under, but spreading this chalky stuff (an expensive procedure, as marl must be mined and brought some distance) was also necessary.

"I have heard that in France they remove the turf, spread twigs and straw and set fire to them, and replace the turf to let it smolder; and this greatly increases the yield of their fields," said Sister Martha.

"That is a true account of a French practice," observed Freemantle, with a hint of an Englishman's contempt for things foreign. "It is also true that there is a great rise in yield. But that method utterly kills the soil after a few years."

"Do we send a pig again as usual to the Friars Minor of Cambridge?" I asked, when we began discussing our charities.

"Maybe we should see how many piglets survive our sow," suggested Freemantle with a smile.

"Perhaps we could just send the money and let them buy their own pig," offered Sister Harley, and that sensible suggestion was approved.

We had been giving the poor at our gate on All Souls a loaf of bread, a slice of cheese and two herrings. Because our situation was improved, it was agreed to give also a loaf of bread, a half-gallon of ale and two herrings on the day of the Last Supper. "Better limit that to no more beggars than there are nuns at Deer Abbey, or you won't be able to get near the gate for the beggars," advised Freemantle. So we did.

There had been some talk about building two tenements in Banbury on land willed to us last year. Master Freemantle had been asked to find out how much this would cost.

"A carpenter to design, supervise and work on the structure would cost 23 shillings, fourpence," he began, and continued, ignoring the collective sharp intake of breath, "a sawyer for ten days to cut wood we are entitled to free from Wychwood, 14 pence; a thatcher for twelve days would be only fourpence a day, but he'd want board, and he'd have three assistants at onepence ha'penney a day. And nails — we'd want 2,000 — would cost two shillings, eightpence, ha'penney —"[vii]

"Stop, stop!" I cried. "After all that expense, we'd still need to pay a bailiff to collect the rents, and have no guarantee the tenants would not burn the place about their ears the first night. I vote no! We should sell the land!" And that, of course, was that.

We did approve the hiring of a plumber to mend a lead gutter where it links our refectory and kitchen, and to reset a few panes of glass in the church at an estimated cost of fourteen pence.[viii]

"My lady, I should warn you that your villein John Deerfield has set enough money aside to buy a Charter of Manumission from you," said Freemantle.

"He'll not do it, I'll warrant," I declared, knowing the man. "He has twice saved his five marks and each time bought land instead of freedom. He's land hungry. He may die the owner of half Lincolnshire, but he'll die a villein rather than spend five marks on something other than land."[ix]

Next we discussed the purchase of a cow for the guesthouse. "We have more frequent visitors of late," noted Sister Martha, "and it would be embarrassing to be out of butter when the bishop comes." I had let her take over some of my duties as Hosteller, and she takes them seriously — as she ought. Hospitality is a major duty of the Benedictine Order.

Under Master Freemantle's guidance, Deer Abbey was growing ever more sturdy and rich —

we'd had an Archbishop over Christmas! — but also, as England grew more restive, there were more vagabonds, more migrants, and more freshly homeless, many of whom sought a night's safe haven with us.

"How much would a cow of sufficient quality cost?" I asked.

"The steward of the Abbey of Wroxton bought a cow for six shillings, sevenpence[x] at the last cow-market in Banbury," noted Freemantle. "I think Austin might get a better bargain. He's a devil for wrangling over prices." Freemantle grinned reminiscently. Austin was sixteen and Freemantle's hand-picked assistant, of half-villein stock, and encouraged by Freemantle to act rather far above his place.

"Very well, send Adam the cowherd and Austin to the next fair."

We were nearing an end of things when the subject of Father John Ising came up. He was vicar of our manor church at South Broughton. He was paid a salary of only three pounds a year, so perhaps we should not have been shocked to hear he was of low moral character and was keeping a leman and had had two children by her. It was decided that Father Hugh should be the one to tell him he is dismissed.

"Where will he go?" asked Sister Harley with unwarranted sympathy.

"I care not!" I replied sharply. "I will not have a priest with a lecherous eye on abbey land! Now, what is the income from the manor church?"

"Nine pounds, last year," said Edward, looking over Sister Harley's shoulder.

"If we offer four pounds salary, we could get a respectable priest to be vicar," I commented.

"An it please you," began Freemantle, in a gentle, formal way I have learned to hear with a modicum of suspicion, "perhaps we could set aside a small piece of manor land around the church for the exclusive use of the vicar. This 'vicarage,' if you will, would allow the vicar to share the problems of the people around him, because he'd have the same ones. And he would be less dependent on the Abbey for his livelihood."

"I never heard of such a thing," I said, surprised. "I will keep our vicar tied firmly to the Abbey, thank you!" 'Vicarage' indeed!

We spent a little more time reviewing perquisites, and adding our temporalities, spiritualities and, finally, alms and chance gifts.

"Devil take arithmetic!" I cried, tossing down my quill. The sun was setting, almost time for Vespers. I barely had time to rinse the ink from my fingers and take my whirling mind to church, to try to ease it in the Pentecostal prayers: "Grant that by the gift of the Spirit right judgment may be ours and we may ever find joy in his comfort."

But all that night my dreams were of tally sticks, unpaid tithes, and the twenty-six shilling salary of Joan, our baker and brewer at Deer Abbey, counted in pennies, over and over.

The Gospel at Chapter Mass next morning contained a sheep parable. I don't find them as charming as I did years ago, when I knew nothing of sheep. It may well be that sheep know the voice of the Master and follow it, but they will likewise follow the bellwether even into a swollen river, and drown.

I sometimes wonder if Our Lord was not making fun of us when he compared us to sheep.

The reading from the Holy Rule that morning in Chapter was on tardiness. "'He who does not come to table before Grace, so that all may say it together and sit down to table at the same time, must be corrected once or twice if this be through negligence or fault. If after this he do not amend, let him not be suffered to share in the common table but be separated from the company of all and eat alone, his portion of wine being taken from him until he makes satisfaction and amends.'"

Father Hugh added a commentary of his own: "Grace is not a word before eating, it is common prayer like all the other offices you pray. In coming late, you interrupt the others, which is rude; and since God hears and answers prayers, you interfere in a dialogue with One whose indignation you should most scrupulously avoid."[xi] He blessed us then and went to his breakfast with Father Piers.

Our daily Chapter meeting continued in an uneventful way. Our novice, Anne Flowers, a winning child of fourteen, was rebuked for singing secular songs while dusting Sir John de Cynegil's effigy in the church. But then Sister Beatrice came forward with a petition to end manual labor.

"We are rich enough now," she argued while three others nodded, "to have servants do all the manual labor. It is not seemly for those of us gently bred to soil our hands with these things."

"I assume you realize you are asking me to break the Holy Rule under which we live?"

"Madame, there is not an abbey of nuns within a day's journey of here that continues the practice of manual labor!"

"There are two abbeys of nuns within a day's journey. One is a collection of ugly merchants' daughters and simple gentlewomen; the other has become a place where students from Oxford stop to take their ease."

"Well, we could do things other than pick apples and sweep floors, could we not?"

"What sort of labor would you do? Copy books? Not one of you four is literate enough for that! Embroider? We already embroider enough albs, chasubles, altar linens and netted purses in a year to stretch from Land's End to John o'Groats!

"It is true St. Benedict lived a very long time ago. I doubt very much if he had this collection of noble daughters in mind when he wrote his Holy Rule. Yet consider this: The Rule stands on three legs: study, labor, and prayer. You who are illiterate cannot study. If we remove labor, there will remain only prayer. And I believe most profoundly that, for sinners such as we, a life of prayer unrelieved by anything else would find us looking forward to death and damnation if only for the change!"

They had the grace to look abashed, and I concluded, "So long as I am abbess, you will labor in God's garden."

"And God grant you long life!" cheered Sister Alison, quite out of turn. But it seemed by the four sullen faces that it might be less joyous to rake hay in the meadow this summer.

I was on my way to my quarters after Chapter when the little bell that hangs outside the cloister door rang excitedly. Its ring signaled the entrance of a male. Since it was on my way, I moved to intercept him and it proved to be old Rolf, the Abbey shepherd, ragged and odorous and indescribably dirty.

"M' lady, wool merchant is here! I saw 'im cast a sort o' wool by shearers and showed 'im way t' guesthouse!"

"Showed him the way? Why, John Fortey knows his way around our inner court as well as I do!"

"Ye'um. But 'im not Mester John. Look a sight like 'im, but too young. Be 'is son, likely."

"Very well. Thank you for showing him the way and for coming to tell me. I will see him shortly. You go back to your sheep."

"Yes, m' lady. Thank 'ee." He gave his forelock a quick tug and was gone.

Hurried preparations to meet our important guest were made. I changed into my best linen habit and new silk veil. At times like this, and at my age, it's good to be a nun: a wimple covers a multitude of wrinkles and gray hair.

"John Fortey has been buying our wool for fourteen years. I thought he would go on forever. I wonder what his son is like. John did mention last year he might send his son."

"Yes, m'lady." Mellie deftly inserted the last pin in my veil, then attached my carved ivory rosary to my belt. My servant is dark and kind and often silent, which made her a blessing.

"Thank you Mellie, that will do nicely. Where's Anne Flowers?" "Waiting at guesthouse, likely, with Lady Martha and Master Freemantle."

"It is time we went there, then," I said, and took up my crozier.

Anne Flowers and Sister Martha stood waiting, encumbered by a silver ewer of warm water, a bowl, a carved wooden box of soft soap, and a fresh linen towel. I led the little procession up the five stone steps to the guesthouse's great hall.

I am proud of our new stone guesthouse. The six windows in the hall have panes of clear glass in the newest fashion, and on this brilliant day the sunlight poured in, lighting up the big room in a marvelous way.

Under a window and near one end of a heavy trestle table stood Thomas Fortey. He did look much like his father, being stocky and of medium height, with honey-colored hair. He was wearing a scandalously short mulberry jupon, its broad pleats held in place by a green belt, the same shade as his hose. He glanced up at us out of his father's piercing blue eyes and bowed low. When he straightened, he was perilously near laughter.[xii]

"My father said you would wash my hands, but I thought all abbeys had given up such old-fashioned customs."

"Master Fortey," I said reprovingly, "if this were truly an old-fashioned abbey, I would wash your feet as well."

He did laugh then, an infectious noise, so that we smiled despite ourselves, and he came forward with a quote — the first of many — to let us wash his hands: "Wash sheep for the better where water doth run, and let him go cleanly and dry in the sun." Mellie held my crozier so I could pour the water myself.

Mellie then took the washing paraphernalia away, and we followed Master Fortey back to the table. He had indeed sampled our wool; there were several clumps of it scattered on the table.

I sat at the head of the table on a heavy chair carved on Gothic lines. Anne and Sister Martha sat on my left; Freemantle on my right. Fortey remained standing, and gathered the clumps of wool, turning them over in a seemingly absent-minded way.

"How is your father, Master Thomas?" I asked.

"Oh, quite well, quite well," he replied. Then with more animation, "Mind you, we thought he was sickening to die during Lent. He' d get up in the morning, take a turn around his garden and go back to bed for the day. Finally, he sent to Almayne for his brass — and that started his recovery."

"How was that, Master Thomas?" asked Anne.

"He wanted a fairly complicated brass, my lady, one foot on a fell and the other on a wool-pack, and there were going to be extra charges, and it was going to take longer than originally estimated, and in the excitement and fury of trying to get what he wanted, my father completely forgot he was dying!" Master Fortey's eyes twinkled and he put on a wise face. "That's what happens when a working man tries to live the life of the idle rich. 'So just thou art, Lord, thy rewards so truly given!' My father is buying wool now in a small way around our neighborhood."

A soft footfall on the stair marked the entrance of Sister Harley, her long white hands clasping a ledger book to her breast. She was so slender and supple that she looked tall, though she was below medium height.

Following close behind her was Edward of Oxford, Assistant Bailiff, young and fair and necessary to Sister Harley because she was quietly, adamantly, fashionably illiterate. He was wearing his best houppeland, a clear blue gown with dagged sleeves.

Master Fortey had turned at their entrance and bowed. He watched Sister Harley slowly cross the room, met her sideways glance of gold-green eyes with an appreciative grin, and sat down.

Sister Harley sat on my right. Edward sat across from her, next to Anne. Master Fortey was further down the table, plucking at a clump of wool, holding it to the light. There was a brief silence.

"My lady," said Master Fortey at last, "your wool appears to be of the highest quality. So it is with regret that I cannot offer the same price as was given for it last year."

This sort of talk was old stuff with me. It meant only that we were about to bargain seriously for our wool.

"Have they discovered a new and ample source for good-quality wool?" asked Freemantle, a trifle sarcastically.

"No, indeed they have not. In fact, Cotswold Fine is becoming rare on the Calais market. These new English clothmakers are buying up a great deal of it. And Lombards — 'may their way be dark and slippery' — buy what they can of the rest. Since England cannot guarantee a good and steady supply to the Netherlands, they turn increasingly to Spain."

"The Spaniards produce a very low-grade wool, don't they?" I asked curiously, though I knew the answer.

"Oh, yes, my lady. But Spain can guarantee delivery, and we no longer can. Therefore, I can but offer you nine marks a sack for your wool."

"It seems to me, Master Fortey," I said, "that a rare and much desired product should be worth more, not less. Say, fourteen marks a sack?"

Fortey made a violent gesture of shock. "'Help me, Lord, for there is no one left who is godly!' My lady, you astonish me. Ten."

I lifted my chin and looked firm. "Thirteen."

"Ten marks, five shillings," he muttered as if it hurt his mouth.

"Twelve." That was last year's price.

"Have mercy upon me Lord, for I am weak!" He thought a moment. "Eleven."

I prayed to the Virgin and stuck by my price. "Twelve marks." There was a pause. "'God dwells within her and she stands unmoved,'" Fortey said at last. "Done, if you can supply a dozen sacks of sufficient packing and true winding, ten fine and two middle, and 25 fleeces."

"Agreed. What wool packer will you send?" This was an important question, because some wool packers can be bribed by the buyer to affirm the wool to be of a lower grade than it is, thus cheating the seller out of an honest price. Of course, a dishonest wool packer can also be bribed to include feathers, stones, hair and other noxious items to make up a seller's shortfall in weight, thus cheating the buyer.

"Would you agree to William Breton?" asked Fortey.

"William Breton should thank the Almighty God every night he has never had to deal with me!" I responded indignantly. Just to agree to Breton could damage one's reputation, and I saw by the pleased light in Fortey's eyes that he liked my answer. I was pleased to see that light.

"'May the word that thou hast spoken stand ever unchanged as heaven.' I understand Breton seeks to buy a general pardon from the king in order to escape prosecution."[xiii]

"I doubt a royal pardon will make him into an honest man," I replied.

"It will save him from the royal prison — or the royal hangman," laughed Fortey. "Of course, he has cheated enough woolmen of their gold that should he come to the Leadenhill wool exchange, his life would not be worth an addled egg."

"Very well, we are agreed about Breton. How about John Byford?"[xiv]

"Agreed. And I will pay one-third when the wool is delivered to Leadenhill, one-third in six months, and one-third in a year's time."

"Nay, Master Fortey, you will pay as your father paid: One-third down, one-third on delivery, and the balance in six months. Agreed?"[xv]

Fortey opened his mouth, closed it, and tried again. "'At thy rebuke, O Lord, both rider and horse lay stunned.' Agreed." He rose and came down the table and held out his hand. I stood and grasped it fervently.

"Wine, Mellie!" I called, and she quickly brought two silver goblets filled with sweet, spiced wine so we could drink to the bargain. I looked over my cup at Master Freemantle, who smiled his approval broadly: his pupil had learned her lessons well.

I turned back to Master Fortey to tell him to keep his cup as a gift. He thanked me. Tracing with a forefinger the grapevine pattern etched into the cup, he said, "My father has a collection of these cups. I trust this is the start of my collection." Then he scowled at me. "But you drive a hard, shrewd bargain for a holy woman of God!" he admonished. Yet his eyes twinkled.

A sudden fear overtook me. "We will be able to supply 25 fells, won't we, Sister Harley?"

She gravely opened her account book, but a helpless expression quickly developed, and she handed the book to Edward. After a moment, he said, "Oh, yes, it looks as if we have at least thirty-two fells."

I turned on Master Fortey and caught him with his mouth open. "Nay, Master Fortey, you have bought all our wool and must leave us a few sheepskins to cover our nakedness this winter."

Fortey laughed, but it was close to the truth. We would have well over twelve sacks of wool, counting desmane, tenant and manor villeins', but we had agreed to sell wool also to an English cloth-maker, and it seemed as if we would sell the last of our wool to him and buy his cloth for ourselves: 'sell the skin for a penny, buy the tail for a groat' — said not of a hard, shrewd bargainer, by St. Loy, but poor foolish me, custodian of empty distaffs and idle looms.

At that moment came the clangorous call of our small frater bell, a noise that would continue until everyone was in her place for midday dinner in the frater.

"We will dine with Master Fortey — including you, Anne," I said, when I saw the novice begin to rise from her place.

"Yes, my lady," she replied, and sat down. Mellie sailed out to tell the kitchen, and advise Sister Alison, our Precentor and third in command, to take my place at the head table.

"Come Anne," said Sister Martha, "sit next to me. We'll let the men have that side of the table to themselves."

"Yes, domina." Anne obeyed with becoming meekness.

We were served sweet pea soup, mushrooms and leeks, chicken blancmange and a wonderful venison umble pie, all with fresh ale.

In a little while, Sister Martha said teasingly, "Master Fortey, you spoke ill of the Lombard. Surely he is a fellow Christian?"

"They're a menace to England!" he growled, setting his goblet on the table with a thump. "Take the Lombard woolman: he offers good prices for the wool he buys — but on very long terms of credit. He will pay a third down and sail away with your wool. He will sell it in Venice for a cash profit and then lend his cash to English merchants at ruinous rates of interest 'thus, if you will believe, wiping our nose with our own sleeve!'"[xvi]

Edward chortled and said, "I believe there is a Lombard in the neighborhood, though we haven't seen him."

"Yes, we have," contradicted Anne quickly, then blushed and was silent. Her expression was guilty, so I asked her to continue.

"My lady, Master Freemantle recently encountered a Lombard and told me of it, and asked me not to tell you."

My indignation was rising. "Master Freemantle does not rule here! You will speak what you know of this!"

Anne came to kneel at my feet. "My lady, you have told me not to spend time in the company of men, but I saw Master Freemantle cutting down that old, crooked apple tree that grows by the wall in our Outer Courtyard and asked him what he was doing. There was no one else near and he told a wonderful story, and we laughed — and then I remembered your command, and I was afraid."

"When did this happen?"

"The fourth Wednesday after Easter, My lady — " said Freemantle, anxiously.

"We will speak more thoroughly of this in Chapter day after tomorrow," I said to Anne. I was reasonably sure the encounter was entirely innocent, but Anne is fourteen and of an age when she should learn to shun the company of men if she is to become a chaste nun. "Take your place again, child," I added and smiled at her.

"Now, Master Freemantle, what of this encounter with a Lombard?"

"It was a misunderstanding, my lady," replied our steward, nervously gearing himself up for a story. "I was riding back to the abbey from Deerfield when a dark man, outlandishly dressed in Lombard style, caught up with me. He was riding a tired white Barb, and said he was very anxious to speak with the Steward of Deer Abbey. He said by very circuitous speech that if he could but meet the man he could offer a deal that would enrich everyone save the King of England — who did not need enriching."

Everyone looked shocked except Master Fortey, who looked thunderous, and Freemantle, who was looking secretive. I was not shocked at the attempt to bribe — Lombards are capable of anything — but that I had not been told of it. More than one abbey has been ruined by a dishonest steward.

"I revealed myself to be the person the Lombard was looking for, and told him I would listen if we could continue our ride back to the abbey — for it was late in the day.

"The Lombard said it was outrageous what was charged foreigners by customs when they exported English wool of the higher grades. What he was looking for was lower-grade wool that would mysteriously upgrade itself once out of the reaches of English customs men. As an act of charity, the Lombard continued, he would be willing to pay Cotswold Fine prices for some of this inferior wool. However, the difference in price between the inferior and superior would be paid under the table, of course.[xvii]

"It happened," continued Freemantle, "the Lombard's English and circumlocution, and my difficulty in understanding, were such that we were nearly home before I was sure I understood. 'But it is the woolpacker, not the buyer or seller, who sets the grade of the wool!' I told him."

"Breton!" growled Master Fortey.

"Precisely," agreed Freemantle. "That is the man the Lombard suggested. Properly bribed, he said, Breton would affirm that Cotswold Fine is Cornish Hair."

I made a sound in my throat, trying to subdue my outrage enough to speak, but Master Freemantle looked at me so guilelessly that I held my peace and nodded at him to continue.

"The Lombard said he could offer two pounds in silver English pence to close the bargain. By this time we were at the gate I invited him to wet his throat, probably dry after so much talking. He agreed and we rode under the gatehouse, and the gate closed behind us.

"We dismounted by the stables and I whistled like this —" Freemantle gave three rising shrill whistles.

"*Oh!*" I said, and began to smile.

"... which the Lombard thought was my call for a servant to take the horses, but which is the signal I give our dogs when there is an enemy to be torn."

"Aaah," said Fortey with a broad grin.

"I did not know a horse as tired as that Barb could throw a man that far," continued Freemantle, indicating a longish arc with one forefinger. "Even when urged to do so by dogs. I did not know a man so encumbered with rich fabric could run so fast. He managed to escape with a whole skin — mostly — but those big padded sleeves and the rear part of his jupon were left behind to amuse the dogs!"

By this point in the tale we were helpless with laughter. Master Fortey was making little crowing sounds and leaning forward over the table. I had bowed my head and covered my eyes, but my trembling shoulders gave me away.

Edward was first to recover enough for speech. "If — if the gate was closed, h-how did the Lombard escape?"

"He swarmed up that apple tree by the wall. That's why I cut it down, so it can't be used as a ladder again. His horse was so terrorized by the dogs we couldn't get near it, so we opened the gate and encouraged it to run out."

Freemantle turned to me. "The reason I asked Lady Anne not to tell you the story is that I was afraid you would not approve of my setting dogs on a Christian — even if he *was* a Lombard."

"Any man who attempts to suborn my Steward deserves to have the fear of the Lord put into him, with dogs or anything else that's handy! Master Freemantle, I wronged you just now. I doubted your loyalty, and after all these years. You are a good man."

"My lady, it is my chiefest ornament to be your servant," said Freemantle, rising and bowing deeply.

"Very pretty!" cheered Master Fortey. He lifted his last fragment of pie to his lips, chuckled one last time, and said, "I'd wager none but the king is so well entertained or well fed as this."

Edward snorted. "I doubt the king has any idea whether he feasts or starves, and whether there is talk or silence."

"Poor man, God save him," I hastily added, trying to mean it and not think of the sins of the grandfather. "I wonder what he'll say when he recovers his wits and sees a strong son for him to bless?"

"Probably that it was born of the Holy Ghost and is no get of his," said Sister Harley in her low, furry voice, running a pale finger around the edge of her cup. "Everyone knows he's been a chaste saint from birth; how could *he* father a son? I heard he ran away when a woman at court showed him her bosom." She lifted her strange golden eyes to Edward, who let his expression show clearly what *he* would do if a woman showed her bosom to *him!*

I felt a sudden grip of anger. I didn't know which was worse, her provocative behavior or his quick and bold response to it. I only knew I wanted to lock them away separately till next St. Geoffrey's Day![xviii] Then I determinedly put away my anger, for who knows what is in the heart of another?

The heavy bronze voice of Adonai, our bell, interrupted our idle talk, calling us to Sext. Fortey humbly asked if he might join us, and I said yes, of course. His mellow voice picked its way nimbly over the prayers, a nice counterpoint to our lighter ones: "... while sinners are rooted out every one, and their graceless names forgotten."

After Sext, Master Fortey announced he had many miles to travel in the seven hours before nightfall, and would not stay longer despite our pleas. So we walked his big, gray horse to the gatehouse, watched him mount, and stood waving until he was out of sight. Then, so long as we were there, we decided to walk along the road and watch the shearers and shepherds.

Shearing meadow was directly across from the abbey gate. Shaped roughly like a triangle, it was broad where it met the road and narrowed as it rose up a low hill to meet a grove of oak trees at its crest. The meadow was bordered by quickset hedges.

Flocks large and small, shorn and unshorn, were scattered over the meadow, but many of the lambs were in a single unhappy group, waiting for their mothers. Near the road a long thatched roof supported on poles gave shade to eight shearers, four men and four women, who with great skill rolled and shifted the passive sheep and, with enormous scissors, clipped away their wool. As each sheep was released, one or two old men caught it and daubed tar on any cuts to keep away scab and flies.

A servant girl in Abbey Livery was waiting to pour water in a cup so the shearers could wet their throats between sheep. A lamb hovered around her skirt and she occasionally knuckled its hard head affectionately.

"That's Jack, our cade lamb," explained Sister Martha, to the appreciative giggles of my ladies.[xix]

"His mother wouldn't have him, but we think he's sweet."

We watched as a freshly shorn ewe, her flank marked with tar, made her way to the hurdles enclosing the lambs, was let in, and selected her own lamb unerringly.

Up and down the narrow, rutted lane we called a road went John Freemantle, resplendent in a gray linen houppeland cut to show off his broad shoulders and hide a small paunch. He was riding a very frisky young bay gelding the Abbey had given him for New Year's. He saw us, nudged the bay into a Canterbury gallop and headed right for us, sliding to a halt barely in time, pulling his rolled-brim black leather hat off and bowing till it nearly swept the ground. It was a very dashing entrance, and my ladies applauded with delight. They crowded round to praise his riding and pet his horse.

"My lady, my ladies!" he announced. "We will shear 650 sheep and have 75 fells as well! There will be no need to request letters patent from the bishop so we may beg in the street!"

There was cheerful laughter at this announcement — which Freemantle made to us every year. We were never in danger of becoming licensed beggars, but Freemantle was reminding us gently this was chiefly his doing.

"What's a fell, Master John?" asked Sister Emma, a very young nun who came to us recently when the little priory of St. Mary's-at-Malling was broken up, and who knew nothing of sheep.

Freemantle stared at her in mock astonishment for so long I thought she would perish of embarrassment, then answered: "A fell is a sheepskin with the wool left on. A piece of a fell is a breckling. A recently-shorn fell is a shorling. A morling is a fell from a sheep found dead — we get Simple Jack to skin *them*. All of them are worth good silver pence. Can you remember that? Pay attention to me and you'll be Bailiff one day."

Freemantle bowed again over the neck of his nervous horse, replaced his hat and let the animal dance him away to resume his supervision of the workers.

We re-grouped and began to walk along the road, watching the work in progress. As we caught the eyes of the shearers or shepherds, they paused only long enough to tug a forelock. They had much to do before sunset.

But my ladies quickly grew bored with the dust of the road and the cut sheep and unhappy lambs and dogs unwilling to come and be petted; and they began to cast longing eyes at the gatehouse.

So we started back, only to be cut off by Freemantle, who wanted a word with me. I walked off the road onto the grass verge beside the abbey wall, and he jumped off his horse.

"My lady," he said, tugging gently at the restless horse's reins to keep it occupied, "There is herriot to be claimed of Edith Longhand."

"*What?!*" I exclaimed. "Tom Longhand dead? How did this happen?"

"He was repairing the thatch on top of their cottage four days ago when a beam broke and he fell through and broke his neck."

"Poor Edith!" My heart went out to the new widow. They were poor, although not the poorest of my villeins. Tom Longhand had brought a hen all plucked and drawn to the Abbey on the Feast of St. Eustace every September 20 for the last five or six years. I remembered him as tall for a villein, with big hands and a tangle of red curls over a bony face. "I must go to Edith at once!" I said.

"Yes, and take herriot."

"Devil take herriot!" I said angrily. I often thought Freemantle a shade callous towards our villeins.

"Nay, madame. We have discussed this before. If you renounce the right to claim herriot in one instance, you may find you cannot claim it in any. And should this Abbey one day be impoverished (as it has been in the past), and should your rich villein John Deerfield die (as one day he must), you may find yourself going hungry for lack of the fat ox you might claim as herriot."

"That is true; I had forgotten your good advice on this subject. Very well, I will go to her tomorrow and claim herriot as you have shown me. I know you are busy with the shearing; will you send Austin?"

"With all the vagabonds and outlaws at large today, you may have need of someone who once practiced with a sword: I'll come myself." He gave a wry smile at this reference to his younger days. "Will you bring the Lady Harley to write down in her book the transaction?"

"Yes and I suppose we must have Edward as well. And I will ask Father Hugh to come along; he is good company and we may need to bless someone."

"Yes, m'lady. With your permission, I will return to my duties." He bowed and, showing off old skills, leaped back into the saddle with a single bound, replaced his hat and trotted off.

I don't like the idea of herriots; a villein's widow in despair over the loss of her helpmate does not need someone stopping by to claim her best beast, even if the law says it is her lord's right. But Freemantle's argument was valid, and I would go on the morrow to see poor Edith Longhand.

I was alone later, washing my hands for supper, when Sister Emma came quietly up to me, looking over her shoulder to be sure we were alone. "My lady," she said softly, dabbling her fingers in the stream of warm water, "is it true what Master Freemantle said? *Could* I be Bailiff if I let him teach me what I need to know?"

"My child, he was teasing you. I try to select the person I feel is most qualified whenever there is a vacancy among my Obedientiaries, and consider yourself: You are as illiterate as a puppy! How could you keep the books?" (For by St. Loy, I would have no more illiterate Bailiffs!)

Sister Emma hung her head, but murmured, "Sister Harley cannot read or cipher, and you made *her* Bailiff."

I dried my hands and turned to her. "Listen carefully to me. Sister Harley is not quite so illiterate as she would appear. It is fashionable for noble ladies to have a secretary to write their letters for them, and Sister Harley has caught the idea from her sisters.

"When she first came here, Harley was a beautiful child with winning ways. Sister Mary, who was Bailiff then, would let young Harley 'help' with the books to tempt her into doing her sums, and they became close friends. Then Sister Mary became very ill. Sister Harley nursed her day and night and was with her when she died.

" Now, Sister Mary's uncle was Sir Richard, and he came to see her before she died. She made him promise to take a special interest in her friend.

"I'm sure you know how important the good will of Sir Richard is to the Abbey in this unfortunate land where the powerless are ever in danger. So when he insisted that Sister Harley be made Bailiff, and offered to pay the salary of an assistant out of his own purse, I could not refuse. Sir Richard remains interested in Sister Harley and, by extension, the entire Abbey."

While Sister Emma was thinking this over, I took down our little whetstone from the lavatory and began to remove a nick in my eating knife's blade I had noticed at dinner. She finally said, "I wish I had a strong knight to be *my* friend."

"You get nothing for nothing, child. Sister Mary died of pox and Sister Harley risked her life to nurse her friend."

After another pause for thought, Sister Emma asked quietly, "Will you teach me to read, Lady Margaret?"

I smiled my approval of the question. "It is flattering of you to ask me. But first you must see if Sister Ann will let you join Anne Flowers' lessons. If our novice is too advanced for you, and if her teacher has no time for special lessons, then I will teach you."

"Thank you m'lady." Sister Emma curtsied. "I will go speak with her at once."

When she was gone Sister Harley appeared as if by magic to wet her fingers. She soaped and rinsed them in silence and dried them thoroughly on the linen towel hung on the wall behind her. There was no sound but the scurf of my blade on the stone. Then, just before she strode noiselessly away, she looked at me with her enormous golden stare and said, "Thank you, my lady."

For what, I wondered.

The next morning, after Mass, we prepared to set out to see the widow Edith Longhand. My white mule was brought to the outer courtyard, his red harness gleaming and brass bells jingling. Sister Harley was helped aboard the ambling gray and Edward climbed nimbly enough up on our dun.

John Freemantle's nervous bay became excited when two dogs began a fight practically under his hooves, and he fell over poor Father Hugh's old donkey — which slyly bit the bay in a tender place during the process of getting untangled. Neither was hurt.

One would have thought we were going on a pilgrimage for all the fuss that was made. All my ladies and half our servants turned out, shouting good wishes and bad advice. We were delayed by the reluctance of our black mare to shoulder the two panniers carrying (too much) food, three kinds of wine, a jug of sweet milk and two gallons of fresh ale.

It was, as Master Freemantle noted, good shearing weather — clear, warm and dry.

Freemantle's wife came forward to bid her husband Godspeed. She was a beautiful woman, tall and strongly built, with thick hair the color of ripe grain.

For all I am a nun, and one who has lived up to her name, I like a good romance — and theirs is true.

Elizabeth was the daughter of a wealthy merchant, and so beautiful her father had hoped to marry her to a knight badly in need of an enormous dowry. John Freemantle's father was also a wealthy merchant and wanted his son to marry into a higher class. But there were other children and there were no serious objections raised when the two began courting. Just in case, however, John and Elizabeth told no one when they plighted their troth.

John's father embarked on a campaign to convince the king and his nobles that the Freemantles should be ennobled, a campaign that impoverished them and proved fruitless.

Elizabeth was locked away in an upstairs room by her father for three months in an attempt to get her to confess the trothplight, revealed when her father tried to arrange another marriage, had been made under duress. It was only after she had not eaten anything for a week that her mother interceded for her, and she was thrown out of the house with nothing but an old wine-colored mantle.

She had no place to go but her in-laws-to-be. They took her in, but begrudged everything they had, of Christian charity, to give her. It was not until Freemantle was taken on as our Steward, two years later, that he was able to send for her. Father Hugh blessed their marriage at our own church door, saying he was sure that, as Elizabeth had been thrown out of her house, God would not mind if she were not married from her own parish.[xx]

Elizabeth lifted her hand to her husband, who kissed it courteously. He touched each of his children (a boy and four girls) on their heads, and our little procession began to move out under our big stone gatehouse. The watchers cheered and waved. Four had climbed to the battlemented roof of the gatehouse and cheered and waved kerchiefs for as long as they could see us. It was hard to believe they knew we'd be home before nightfall.

The winding road dipped to the ford of the stream called Abbey River, then rose slightly and entered Wychwood. There the atmosphere changed, and our mounts moved more alertly and cautiously. Enormous trees cut off most of the sunlight, making a green twilight, very pleasant after the harsh glare of the open road.

Edward took up a post in front and Freemantle brought up the rear. Knowing the royal forest to be the hiding place of outlaws, their weapons, especially Freemantle's experienced sword, were a comfort.

Sister Harley looked around with a speculative air and asked, "*Was* there ever a witch in Wychwood?"

Freemantle smothered a laugh. I replied, "I think not. The forest is called Wychwood because there are a great many elm branches suitable to cut for bows. Wych is another way of saying *wick*, which means green and supple. I will admit, however, that there are those who will try to make you believe some silly superstition about a witch in this forest."

Sister Harley was scandalized. "Are you saying you do not believe in witches?"

"Of course not. Did I not see with my own eyes the lead image of the king made by Jaquetta, Duchess of Bedford, with which to work her evil spells? It is displayed by the nuns at Sewardsley as a lesson and warning that even our nobility is not free from the devil's taint."

We all crossed ourselves and rode in silence for a while. Then Father Hugh changed the subject.

"Master Freemantle, now that Deer Abbey has acquired the recent perquisite to take two beasts of the forest a year from Wychwood, I have been trying to learn something about hunting. Free Warren, which right we have had since the time of Henry II, and has put many a rabbit into our pot,[xxi] covers all small game. The "beasts of the forest" are listed as the wild boar, the red deer, and the fallow deer. My question is, where does the roe deer fall? Is it not also a beast of the forest? Is its flesh not good to eat? Or is it poor game to hunt?"

"Nay, father, the roe deer leads the gazehounds on a merry chase once the liam hound has started him, and his flesh and umbles make a feast fit for any palate. But the roe deer is jealous of his forest, and wherever he establishes himself he drives off all other deer. Moreover, he likes a good distance between himself and others of his kind, so where he is, hunting is poor. King Edward III removed him from the list of beasts of the forest, to the rejoicing of the villeins, who can hunt him with impunity."

Then to me: "My lady, now that we can hunt the deer and boar, are you going to acquire a pack of dogs?" His voice betrayed a hint of hope.

"I think not, Master Freemantle. Surely to follow the hunt is a noble — and secular — thing to do, not an occupation for holy nuns of the cloister. And since we are to take only two beasts of the forest a year, hardly worth the expense. I think we will continue to ask Sir Richard's son to lead the chase with his dogs. He greatly enjoys the hunt."

"Yes, m'lady."

"You will, of course, represent the Abbey by appearing in the chase whenever possible."

"Of course, m'lady. Thank you, m'lady." And he made his horse dance thrice across the lane.

There had been a scent of pigs for some little while, and now the source was revealed. In a clearing just coming into sight were two small, neatly-made buildings with low thatch roofs. Beside and around one were about two dozen spotted pigs, some shuffling and rooting in the earth after the manner of their kind, but the rest intently watching the goings-on by the other house, where eight or nine villeins were gathered. An old man, evidently the owner of the pig farm, was standing in front of his door, winding up a speech. We could not hear the words, but there were cheers and laughter at the end.

Then the old man went inside, but immediately came back out again, to say a few more words. He had left his door open and gripped the latch in one hand. A young man stepped forward, took the latch and went inside. The old man said a few more words, then knocked at the door. It was opened promptly, and the old man assumed the pose and gestures of a beggar asking for food and a place to sleep. The young man gave him warm welcome, the two went inside, and the crowd began to disperse.

"What was that?" asked Sister Harley. "What did it mean?"

"That is a very old ceremony marking the turnover of a holding by a villein to his heir. They've been through the legal procedure at Sir Richard's manorial court, where the old man released his holding and his son paid his fine for entry. But this second ceremony comes from the old ways, and lets the neighbors know the young man is now in charge. Probably the old man was ready to retire and the young one wants to marry."

"They do not marry hereabouts," added Freemantle, "until they have the means to support a wife and children. If the old man had not relinquished his living, it would have meant a late marriage for the son — and possibly a rise in the number of bastards in the area. Their problem now will be to keep the old man from interfering in the running of the holding."

"Now, Master Freemantle," objected Father Hugh gently, "These people tend to think the old ways are best. Most of these arrangements work out well."

"Fascinating," sneered Edward, urging his horse forward. As if it weren't, as if anything not noble were of no interest, an irrelevancy instead of one of the bits of color that make up the tapestry that is the world we live in.

Father Hugh began absently to whistle an air and we one by one joined in the song: "Never had the apple taken been, the apple taken been; Never had our Lady been heaven's queen ..."

Talk drifted onto various topics: "If, when an angel takes on some tangible form to appear to a human being, it looks as beautiful as our artists try to portray it, why does his first saying always have to be, 'Fear not'?"

"That pig overlaid four of her young last year, too, as I recall."

". . and Canute rebuked the sea, but the tide came in anyway and got the hem of his gown all wet..."

There was some friendly disagreement: "Nay, the abbeys in England are mostly all right —save in the north, of course, where disease, poverty and the marauding Scots combine to make normal conditions impossible."

"Now, now, John Senoke ruined two nuns with disgusting ease while staying at Easbourne —and that's in *Sussex!*"

"My dear Lady Margaret, that was nearly a hundred years ago! There have been nuns whose virtue was easily lost since the time of Bede, anyway."

"Well, if you want something closer to home and more recent, how about our own Sister Maud, who ran off with that harper to Newcastle-on-Tyne ten years ago?"

"She came back, didn't she?"

"Yes, but only because he was always getting drunk and beating her."

And so on.

We were not far from our goal when Master Freemantle called a halt for dinner. Father Hugh, as usual, took charge of the picnic, rummaging in the panniers, dropping the butter pot and breaking it, burning his fingers in the fire and cutting the spinach pie with the careless art of a chirurgeon.[xxii] But as he enjoyed these self-assigned duties, which included cleaning up and packing things away, no one was willing to spoil his fun.

Then we stood in the cathedral God had built with his own hands, and said the prayers and sang the hymns of Sext. "Grant light when falls our eventide, Life knowing no decay of age, And glory that shall ever bide, A holy death's eternal wage."

I suppose a symptom of age's decay is the difficulty I had in rising after sitting on the ground. But after standing through Sext I was limber enough to climb on my mule with only a little help, and once in the saddle, all was well.

The Longhand place was located on the edge of the forest, on South Broughton Manor land. It was a single structure of two rooms, one for the animals and the other for the humans who lived there. Four people stood outside the building's only door, alternately waving and bowing.

The widow Edith was a short, wiry person of less than thirty years, though her face was lined and her black hair well streaked with gray. A girl with bright red tangled curls, nearly as tall as her mother, watched us warily. A boy of perhaps twelve, dark and thin, stood near his sister. A redhead of four or five pointed at us and yelled, "*I see 'um!!*" They were all wearing faded blue homespun, much patched and torn, and all were rather dirty.

As soon as I was close enough, I pulled to a halt, tumbled off my mule, and hurried to take Edith Longhand into my arms. We wept together some little while, the children whimpering around us, and sympathetic sniffing coming from the background.[xxiii]

After a while Edith broke away from me and knelt and kissed my hand. "You be a good mistress to us," she said. "No doubt you be hot from your ride. Come in; I've a cool drink o' water for you."

The half of the structure meant for human beings was relatively clean, if dark and redolent of the animals living on the other side. A sick piglet and a broody hen occupied baskets near the open fire in the center of the room. I was shown to a stool near the fire.

The water was cool and sweet, served in a clean pottery mug, only a little chipped. The children gathered around to be introduced: shy Nesta, 13, who was to be married summer after this to Alf the smith; proud Bran, 11, who was the man of the family now and doing nearly a man's work about the place; and little Jamie, four, who was variously described as small and wretched, bright as a new penny, and more trouble than he was worth.

Edith Longhand said it was time to look at the animals. She asked me to go outside and to please take Jamie with me. "We got a boar would bite 'im half in two and have 'im for supper, could he ketch 'im." Jamie paled at this, and came obediently with me outside.

We were then treated to a little parade: A cow and a heifer, two ewes and a sickly ram, an enormous sow with a dozen suckling piglets, (which caused me to look significantly at Master Freemantle), and a white boar so immense, vicious and hairy I wondered if he hadn't been stolen from the forest.

I carefully conferred with Father Hugh, Master Freemantle, Sister Harley and Edward of Oxford before announcing my choice. "We need a cow for our guesthouse, a good producer who is gentle and reliable, and not too old. I therefore choose the cow."

Bran and Nesta exchanged looks and sighs. They had wanted me to choose the boar, in order to watch Master Freemantle try to lay hold of it.

But I went to the cow, took the rope halter and turned its head away from the other animals. Then I halted as if in perplexity. "If we take this cow with us, it will be long after dark before we are home," I said, as if just realizing it.

I looked around at the Longhand family's delighted faces. Like all villeins — like all of us — they loved mummery. "It seems to me," I continued in a high voice, "that money would be easier to carry than this cow would be to lead. Tell me, Master Freemantle, what would you guess to be the worth of my cow?"

He swept his expert's eye down the creature's length. "About a penny, m'lady," he answered. (Two years ago Freemantle had come up with this "one-penny-solution" to the herriot problem.)

"Tell me, Edith Longhand, would you buy my cow from me for a penny and save me a journey in the dark?" I asked.

"A penny, a penny!" shouted Jamie. He dashed into the house ahead of his mother and stuck close by her side when she returned, a shining silver penny in her palm. "Abbot of Tewkesbury's servant gave me that for a dozen fresh eggs last Saturday at market," she explained, handing me the coin proudly.

"This is a new-minted coin; and so beautiful that I think I will put it into the hoard we're making to build a new church," I said, putting it into my purse carefully, while Edith beamed with pleasure.

Freemantle began to cast obvious looks at the sun and lengthening shadows, so I asked the last question: "Is there anything we can do for you before we leave?"

Edith dropped at once to her knees, and I thought she would ask for Father Hugh's blessing. "You come to claim herriot as is your right, and out o' love didn't claim it proper, and God bless you. But I want you to take my best beast. You saw 'im and didn't think to claim 'im. I want you t' claim Jamie."

"By St. Loy, Edith! Do you know what you are saying?! You are speaking of a child, not a beast! You cannot be serious!"

"Ah, but I am," said Edith beginning to weep. "The priest said a child must be six afore it can reason. He said an infant can't sin, no more than a beast." Edith painfully made herself stop crying, the better to argue her point.

"Jamie is the cunningest child I ever did see. He wants schoolin' and I got none to give 'im. You could make 'im a priest. You could give 'im a chance t' make us proud of 'im. If he stays here, he'll be just another villein — if he lives, as so many do not."

She began to weep again. The child wandered over to her, and she clutched him to her shoulder and kissed him over and over. "*Will* you take'im?" she asked.

I felt a great fear at this. What should I do? When I looked at Master Freemantle, he was looking as dumbfounded as I felt.

"Father Hugh, what do you advise?" I asked.

He thought a moment. "Let God decide. Go near to where the child is standing, and kneel as his mother is doing. Hold out your arms and say his name. God will put into his head what he should do." And he crossed himself and began to pray silently.

So I did as I was advised. I knelt and held out my arms and said "Jamie," not in a summoning tone, but gently. And he immediately left his mother and came to bury his face in my wimple. I cannot say I was pleased; he was *very* dirty. But this was something so like a miracle that I allowed him to mar its snowy whiteness as much as he would.

Then I picked him up, stood, and faced his mother. "This is not of my doing," I assured her.

"It be God's will," she agreed tearfully. I noticed Bran looking pleased and it occurred to me that with

Jamie gone and Nesta married, Bran was sole inheritor of the place. I was suddenly sure this whole business of Jamie-as-herriot had been Bran's idea.

"I will see to it that Jamie rides to market those Saturdays anyone from Deer Abbey goes, so you may see him there; and you may visit him at the Abbey whenever you wish."

Edith had risen, her face still sad. "I thank you," she said with that terrible dignity the bereaved can attain. "He will make you glad you took 'im in."

We left for the Abbey then, Jamie riding across Freemantle's pommel. Before we had gone a mile, Jamie had caused the bay to rear twice by pulling suddenly on the reins, had spooked all our mounts by shrieking happily at the sight of a deer, and had bitten Freemantle on the thumb when he clapped a hand across the little villein's mouth.

"James Longhand, if we survive this ride back to Deer Abbey, I will draw and quarter you on arrival!" swore the exasperated steward.

"Nay, Master Freemantle," objected Father Hugh mildly, "not James Longhand, James *Herrio*t. Let his new life begin with a new, and appropriate, name."[xxiv]

"Oh, dear," sighed Edward, Assistant Bailiff, shaking his golden locks, "*how* are we going to enter this on our books?"

Sister Harley began to giggle, and shortly we were all laughing, James Herriot loudest of all.

The next morning, scrubbed to within an inch of his life, properly dressed in a tunic from the guesthouse, combed and warned thoroughly, James lasted at Prime only until "Open the gates where right dwells; let me go in and thank the Lord!" before his incessant chatter made me take him out.

He continued speaking in the cloister, so loudly his voice echoed like a bell, until I took him into the orchard to seek relief. His noise stopped at once. At home in the forest, the orchard was almost familiar to James.

We began to walk around. I tried to teach the Pater against the adamantine of his disinterest and the overwhelming competition of the beautiful morning. Then we heard the piping voice of Old Ganfer, our gardener.

Suitably warned, James cooperated in the stealth as we slipped up to see what was happening. Ganfer was stooped over near the end of his row of seven beehives. As we came closer, we could see a twinkling brownish mass clinging to the last hive but one — a swarm of bees. The last hive was new and empty; Ganfer was trying to persuade the swarm to enter its new home. As he crooned to them, he was fumbling with his fingers in the grass, picking something up.

The swarm began to lift in flight. Immediately Ganfer tossed pebbles — which is what he had been searching for in the grass — through the swarm onto the new hive. "Alight, victorious ladies, descend to earth," we heard him mutter in outlandish English. "Fly not into the forest. Be as mindful of my livelihood as God is of His creation." The ancient charm — for such it was — worked. The bees followed the pebbles down to the new hive and began to crawl all over it. When they found the entrance and began to explore the interior, Ganfer straightened stiffly. And saw us watching.[xxv]

"M'lady," he piped in his uncertain treble, touching his forehead. "And who might little Mester be?"

"I be no mester!" laughed Jamie. "I be *Jamie!* Herriot, that's me! Come to stay!"

Old Ganfer looked at me inquiringly, and I quickly explained the circumstances of Jamie's arrival. "... so I suppose he is a sort of herriot. Only I think we might have been better off to have taken any of the other beasts, even that sick old ram."

"Make a priest of 'um?"

"Oh yes, I should think so. He seems bright enough. If he turns out well, we may even find him a place at court, as a clerk."

"M'liddy, m'liddy!" shouted Jamie.

"James, you must learn not to shout. My ears are covered, but I can hear perfectly well. And you should say 'my lady' not 'm'liddy.'"

Jamie visibly gathered his wits and whispered, "M-m-m-my lu-lady."

"Yes, James, what is it?"

"I smell cookin'."

"So do I. Shall we return to the cloister?" "Race 'ee!" shouted the child and was gone.

A little later that morning James was formally introduced to my ladies at Chapter. He had yet to show any sign of homesickness or shyness. He so charmed my ladies I could see they might easily make a pet of him, and I warned them against that. "He is meant for the priesthood," I said, "and possibly a place at Court. We must keep those goals always in mind." I thought the accomplishment of these goals would be a fitting reply to the smug look on Bran's face when he successfully made his mother send James away from his home.

I was on my way to my quarters after turning James over to Sister Lucy for some schooling — the only prayer he seemed to know was "God 'a' mercy!"

which he used as an expletive — when Sister Martha stopped me to confer about the annual Deerfield Fair. Some new booths were proposed; the increased size would draw jugglers, cutpurses and other riff-raff. Sister Martha came with me to intercept a male visitor, who turned out to be Father Piers, Father Hugh's deacon and assistant. He bowed his tonsured head just slightly to us (he was a very dignified man), and kept his hands tucked well into his sleeves.

"Sir Richard is in the guesthouse," he announced, to our dismay, "washing away travel stains. He says he is on his way home from York and is sore hungered. I have supplied him with a fresh gown from the guesthouse closet, but there seems to be no one in the kitchen."

"I loaned the guesthouse staff to the Abbess of Godstow to feast her shearers, who finish today," said Sister Martha.

"Has Sir Richard many with him?"

"Four men-at-arms in livery."

Thank God he hadn't brought a young army with him. "Have we got changes of clothes for them also?"

"Yes, m'lady."

"Very well. They can dine with us in the misericord. We'll delay dinner if we have to until they are ready. They'll sit at the head table, of course, with me and Sister Ann. Bring them there; we'll be waiting."

"Yes, m'lady." He gave that little bow and departed without haste. How odd, I thought; he's beginning to go gray. He was always such a young man!

I turned to Sister Martha, who was this week's reader at meals. "I don't think The Pearl we've been reading is suitable for Sir Richard," I said. "What do we have by way of something secular?"

She thought a moment. "Our alliterative *Morte Arthure* — no, that's too long and too critical of chivalry. We also have *Sir Orfeo*, which is shorter and nicer. Would that be all right?"

"Yes, *Sir Orfeo* is just the thing. I must go change and find my crozier. Send Anne for your book; you go tell the cook there are an extra five for dinner — with men's appetites."

"She'll rage and weep!"

"Let her, so long as she manages to serve all of us."

Sir Orfeo was a success. The story of a knightly hero who restored harmony to his life and kingdom through an act of courage, and was all the while a paragon of chivalry, struck the right note with Sir Richard and his retainers.

The meal was a success, too: soup of leeks and almond milk, a boiled spinach dish with eggs and cheese, young peapods quick-fried in butter, and (best of all) roast venison with a cinnamon-pepper sauce.

"Your son brought us this deer, Sir Richard," I said.

His frown was instant. "From *our* deer park?"

"Nay, sire. We are now allowed the perquisite of taking two beasts of the forest a year from Wychwood, and as we have no dogs and only our Steward has hunting skills, we asked Sir John for help. He said he was pleased to fetch us a deer, so long as it was not from your park." He laughed then and when I added, confidentially, that we planned to make Sir John a pair of gloves from the hide, his mood became pleasant. Talk came around to plans by the Abbey to lease some land on condition the tenant plant an orchard — from which would come the rent.

"I know a man so skilled with grafting he can make a quince grow on pear stock," said Sir Richard. "I will send him to you."[xxvi]

He turned his attention to the sweet just arriving, a strawberry pudding with pomegranate seeds. Then, holding the cup of spiced wine served with it, he rose to speak.

"My ladies, a toast." His retainers rose, looking a little uneasy. "England is unhappy, because its king is ill. Wicked men have taken control of the government and they strip the people of their goods. *Our* king would not stand for that, if he had the power to do anything about it."

Who is this "*our* king" he speaks of? Oh, dear, I like this not! "So here's to our Lord King Henry, who, as sure as he is the true king, will toss those rascals out on their collective ear as soon as he recovers his senses! *The King!*" Cups were raised all over the room, and Sir Richard sat down, looking defiant.

My heart was beating too rapidly. Did Sir Richard think that because I was an aunt of the Duke of York I would countenance treason spoken in my cloister? We well knew those "rascals" were King Henry's dearest friends; he would never throw them out. Who was the "true king"? Not the Duke of York. King Henry had a son; the Duke was not even his heir any longer. I was all amazed. Dared I speak? What could I say? The shire was a hotbed of Lancastrian support; I was by blood a Yorkist. Sir

Richard and the king were my two protectors — and the king lay witless at Windsor.[xxvii]

My fear must have showed plainly on my face, for Sir Richard took my hand and said, "It will be well soon, my lady. You will not be involved unless you choose to be. What was said here today was not understood by a quarter of your nuns, and need not go beyond this cloister."

"You have always been good to us Sir Richard," I gasped, and, to my astonishment, began to cry. Immediately, Sister Harley came from her place and began to wipe at my tears with her handkerchief, and Sister Martha gave me several rather strong blows on the back, and then Sister Lucy nearly choked me by forcing a large dollop of wine down my throat; and my annoyance put a quick end to my tears.

"Enough! Enough! Sit down in your places! I am quite recovered!"

Before the hubbub had settled, the bell rang for Sext. A moment of standing silence was followed by Grace and then I began the 51st Psalm: "Have mercy upon me, O God, after Thy great goodness," with Sisters Ann, Lucy, Elizabeth, Harley and Maud chiming in, "according to the multitude of Thy mercies, and do away my offenses."

My other six ladies and Anne Flowers began the second verse as we marched out of the door to our church: "Wash me thoroughly from my iniquity, and cleanse me from my sin."

Sir Richard and his men joined us, their deep voices uncertain of the words, but respectful. In the church they remained west of our choir and with many signs of the cross prayed with us. One man did wander off to examine the tomb of Sir Richard's father. It was made of carved stone with a fine marble effigy of the old man, and if it rather flattered him, why not? He was a good soul.

As for Sir Richard and his involvement with the Duke of York, and my involvement with them, I could only take comfort in a verse for the season, "The Spirit who is to befriend you, will make everything plain, alleluia." Amen.

Deliver Us from Evil

by

Margaret

of Shaftesbury

1470: The World in Brief

Yoshimara (of the Clan Ashikaga) has built his Silver Pavilion and lives there as Shogun with a brilliant group of artists. Meanwhile, Japan is divided into two warring camps and the Onin War is ravaging the country.

The great European exploration (and exploitation) of Africa has begun. The Portuguese will found San Jorge d'el Mina on the Guinea coast next year.

Abu Said, last of the Timurid (Tamerlane) dynasty, died last year. The Turks and the Venetians have been fighting since 1463. This year a huge Turkish fleet took Euboea from Venice, and since then control Levantine waters.

Ivan III (the Great), is first national sovereign of Russia.

Lorenzo and Giuliano de' Medici continue the rise of the family. They have nearly the power and wealth of princes, but no titles.

Paul II is Pope, a Venetian who began the famous Corso horse races. He is rich, kind and handsome, a collector of jewels and carvings.

Isabella of Castile and Ferdinand of Aragon were married last year, uniting their kingdoms.

Louis XI (the Spider) is King of France. This year he concluded a treaty with the Swiss in a move against Charles the Bold of Burgundy.

It is August 15, 1470, and the War of the Roses is raging in England. George Duke of Clarence and Earl Warwick managed to capture the King last year, but could not keep him. They are now in France, plotting an invasion. August 15 is a holy day, and the villeins have been mostly idle all day. About an hour before sunset it began to rain heavily, and a Duke (with twenty men) has sought shelter at a small abbey of nuns. Having warmed and dried himself, the Duke has put on the rich clothing he loves and is about to meet the elderly abbess, to whom he is distantly related.

Deliver Us From Evil

We all knelt as he entered the room, the sad black of our Benedictine dress offset by our shining faces and shy smiles. He was a small, muscular young man, with the lasting marks of severe childhood illness about his eyes. He was very richly dressed in murrey velvet, the sleeves slashed to show the white silk lining.[xxviii]

He walked slowly across the great hall of our guest-house, golden strands in his dark hair catching and reflecting the candlelight, as did the many gems on his fingers. We had lit tens of candles against the stormy night, and the room was filled with their warm, molten glow. His eyes moved quickly from table to candlestand to nun, taking in the room in a series of glances. His thin mouth half smiling, he absently removed and replaced a ruby ring on his little finger.

He was used to better accommodations, and worse, than this, being both a prince of the blood and a soldier. I noted his herald standing proud and motionless by the door, a man of the north by his dress; and I wondered what it was about this slight young duke that inspired loyalty in such hard men as they.

He had been on his way to Oxford when bad weather and then darkness overtook him, so he stopped (with twenty men) at Deer Abbey. There was in the background of this apparently quiet moment of greeting such a panicked scurrying and turning-out and changing of sheets and strewing of sweet herbs and desperate culinary innovation as is only to be expected when a surprise visitor turns out to be the King's brother.

When he drew close to me, I studied the white roses embroidered on his cloth shoes a moment before I dared raise eyes to his face. He smiled then and held out his hands to raise me to my feet. He kissed my cheek and called me Aunt — for my father was his great-grandfather. It was the Feast of the Assumption and my seventieth birthday, and I was prepared to consider this visit a surprise gift to mark the day.

He was an appreciative guest. He had good things to say about the cooks' efforts, both that night and the next morning. He did not appear at midnight for Matins and Lauds, but did come at dawn for Prime. He was familiar with the prayers ("Almighty Lord and God, who hast brought us to the beginning of this day, keep us throughout its course, that we may not turn aside to sin ..."), which he said sincerely if without great fervor.

After Prime I ordered that his men might replenish their supplies without stint from Abbey storage and cellars. While they were about this, Austin, our acting Steward, gave our noble guest a quick tour. Later Austin complained that the man had not stuck to the usual banalities, but had asked some very pointed questions. "He missed nothing, Madame," he reported. "I think he wishes we trusted not so much to our walls for security."

The Duke and his party were ready to leave well before Terce[xxix] that morning. "My good lady Aunt," he said with that faint smile of his, as he swung a leg over his saddle, "you seem to have things well in hand here, considering your Steward abandoned you to care for my horses a few months ago. I am sure John Freemantle would send warm greetings to you, and tender ones to his wife and children, if he had known we would see you. His absence does you harm — have you friends here? This area is a Lancaster stronghold."

I stood close to his horse's shoulder. "My Lord, there are the de Cynegils. Lady Bertille and I are fast friends these seventeen years. Sir John is our special protector, but he is with the King's army."

"Sir John de Cynegil? So this is his bailiwick. I have heard good things about him. I am sorry we cannot spare him to you."

"Lady Bertille and I will aid one another to the best of our poor womanly ability," I said in conventional reply.

His lip twitched. "If Lady Bertille matches her husband, all will be well with you." He removed a heavy gold and enamel ring from a gloved thumb and bent to give it to me. "I know we have sorely depleted your stock of food and other goods," he said. "This should bring enough to compensate you. If there is any over, consider it a gift to the Abbey."

"I — I thank your grace!" I stammered, overwhelmed, and pushed the ring over my own thumb for safekeeping. Thoughts of our collection of unredeemed tally sticks[xxx] made me feel doubly touched by his determination to leave unhurt those he encumbered with his presence. "You are too generous — we were honored —" I was floundering for words.

"You have done us a service, my Lady," he interrupted kindly. "I shall not forget how you spread a table for me in the midst of my enemies." He smiled a boy's smile — he was only seventeen —

and glanced at my crozier, which is, after all, a shepherd's crook. "If you are in trouble in future, send word to me. You have my ear." He turned his horse away.

I had become gradually aware that his shoulders were very unequally muscled, a defect disguised by padding. I had come also to recognize an unyielding spirit in him that would probably cause him trouble in the years ahead. Suddenly I was aware of a rush of maternal feeling for him, a wish that all might go well with him — a feeling that left me surprised and a little shaken — as with a great clatter he and his men rode out under the gatehouse. We did not, of course, ever see him again. I looked around and saw servants and villeins standing idle. "Sister Harley, set these people to work! Yesterday was the holiday!"

"Yes, my lady. Austin! Come here!"

As I slowly walked back to the inner courtyard — my rheumatism was very painful that morning — my ladies crowded around to see the ring Richard of Gloucester had given us. I hadn't looked closely at it, but was not surprised to trace an enamel image of his badge, the White Boar, on its flat surface.[xxxi] What did astonish me was that I could not get it off. The middle joint on my thumb was swollen with rheums and so excruciatingly painful I could not force the ring over it.

"Never mind, my lady," said Sister Emma gently. "Wear it for a day or so, and it will come off of itself."

"No! I am so proud of his visit, of his calling me Aunt!" I said fiercely. "Such pride as I would feel to wear this ring must not be allowed! I must not wear it!" But it would not come off, and by the time I had reached the inner gate, I had perforce consented to leave it be. Fortunately, it was on the left thumb, and so impeded me little.

After Sext I went to my quarters to search for a counted-thread embroidery pattern Lady Bertille had loaned us, and while there Sister Alys brought Austin to me.

"My lady," he said, using a painstaking bow our missing Steward had obviously taught him, and tugging at his faded red tunic, "the wheat in our desmane fields is nearly ready to be harvested." He held out a small bouquet of the golden grain, the tops bent under the burden of ripe ears. I took the stalks from him — I have seen the harvest for sixty-five years from our fields and know a thing or two about wheat.

"It appears ripe, surely," I said, thumbing a grain out of an ear. "The rain last night did not beat it down?"

"A little, but it will be standing again tomorrow. If we wait beyond Monday we will lose some. The ears will begin to fall of themselves where it is ripest."

"Do our villeins know the harvest will begin soon?"

"Yes, m'lady." Austin flushed darkly and added, reluctantly but scrupulously, "It was Hodge our Reeve who brought me that sample of wheat and reported the state of the grain. We are agreed that it will be an abundant harvest, and it will take two or more bid-reap days in addition to the usual work time to get it all in."[xxxii]

"Be sure the ox for the harvest home feast is fat. These are hard times for our villeins, harder than for the rest of us, and we must give them all their due. They have been good to us."

Austin identified our particular local source of hard times without difficulty. "It would be to everyone's good if we could somehow contain Sir Ranulf! I was standing beside the lane with Hodge when that black-avised bully rode by with his henchmen, and poor old Hodge, trembling like a beaten dog, bowed and tugged his forelock most humbly. I reminded him that he was not Sir Ranulf's villein but ours, and an important man in Deerfield Village; but he said to keep one's house and daughter intact, a little bow was a small price. My lady, surely it is long past time we did something!"

Austin's impatient anger distressed me, but I was old and fearful of strong action. Many problems take care of themselves if left alone. Or Sir John might come home soon and take care of Sir Ranulf as the de Cynegils had for centuries taken care of Abbey problems. Besides, I added aloud, "Sir Ranulf has a powerful friend in the Viscount Peccafortier, which makes it difficult and dangerous to thwart him. Yet one day he will overstep himself, his comeuppance shall come, and he must 'drink to his oysters.' A little patience, Austin, I ask of you."

He ran his fingers through his thick blond hair, and said it must be as I wished, and departed. I heard him mumble something about hoping to fill Sir Ranulf's cup for that drink as he went out.

At supper that night, the talk was all of the visit of Richard of Gloucester: his every word, his clothing, his mannerisms, his preference among the dishes he ate, the good manners of his chestnut stallion, his northern accent, the probable value of the gold ring still stuck on the left thumb of our lady abbess — "Hold, *enough!*" I cried. "Is *nothing* else worthy of conversation?"

After a pause: "There was a fire at Chimneys today," offered Sister Clare meekly. Chimneys was a small de Cynegils manor near us.

"A fire?" I asked sharply.

"Just a little one, my lady," said Sister Harley quickly. "Robyn Bodrey climbed to the top of the bell tower when we told him we saw smoke, and he said it looked to be a small outbuilding."

"It would not surprise me to learn Sir Ranulf started that fire," said Sister Mildred firmly. Sir Ranulf had recently resurrected an old claim to Chimneys, and was pressing it with his usual wholehearted ferocity.

"He wouldn't burn down a place he wanted for himself!" objected Sister Harley.

"He wasn't trying to burn it down. Probably he just wanted to scare away any servants Lady Bertille is keeping there. She herself is at Dowse Manor, I believe?" Sister Mildred looked inquiringly at me.

"Yes, she is supervising the work of remodeling the main house."

"Well, Dowse is right the other side of Wychwood; a perfect time for Sir Ranulf to take possession of Chimneys." Sister Mildred looked satisfied with her chain of logic.

"You think he would just ride in and take possession? Even Sir Ranulf isn't *that* wicked!" objected Sister Caterine, who has a delicate conscience.[xxxiii]

"*All* that family's wicked," replied Sister Mildred, who is my sturdy Chamberlain and flinches at nothing.[xxxiv] "Why, it is generally known that Sir Ranulf's father poisoned his wife, and I have heard that a relation of the family was burned piecemeal upon a stage in Burgundy for a murder so hideous its details should not be told to gentle women!"

Fortunately the bell for Vespers rang at that moment and I was saved from forcing the conversation again into another channel. Discussions like these made me consider re-instituting the Rule of Silence.

My aching bones made sleep come hard that night. Mellie finally gave me a small cup of Water of the Queen of Hungary, which has a hot, harsh taste, but is an excellent remedy for the pains of rheumatism. Dr. John le Spitelman of Oxford came to treat me and had suggested a round of purging and then cautery. I told him I had been very ill with vomiting last year and my rheums pained me the while; and that if he dared poke me with his red-hot irons I'd have him dropped head-first over the marshy side of the Abbey wall! When he saw I was quite serious, he said that perhaps I should try a distillation of three parts *aqua vitae* and two parts rosemary, a concoction invented by Queen Elizabeth of Hungary. I have kept some by me ever since.[xxxv]

The medicine sent soothing warmth into my bones and I lay back gratefully on my bed. As I waited for sleep to overtake me I thought of Sir Ranulf Fitzralph. He was barely twenty-four, but already had a long career of felonious behavior. At age twelve he began by beating a serving maid half to death. A few years ago he came into his inheritance of three small manors and sharply increased his activities. His protector, a Lancaster Viscount, was, of course, no longer welcome at court, but the Yorkist King's long arm did not yet reach into the Cotswolds, so Sir Ranulf was allowed by his protector to intimidate or suborn any juries summoned against him, and, encouraged by immunity, went ever on to greater violence. He would go out of his way to do a wicked thing, and was as thorough in his petty cruelties as in his grosser ones. His Uncle John had been the same way, and there were old tales told about his great-grandfather, who displayed the same traits. Both uncle and great-grandfather came to bad ends, and so would he — soon, I prayed.

As I began to drift into sleep at last, I smiled in recollection of Sister Harley, who had made an edifying prediction of Sir Ranulf's death, saying there would be so many devils squabbling for possession of his soul that not a single angel could get near enough to claim it.

As Cellarer, Sister Harley was in charge of lay labor, and had lately developed a deep concern for the welfare of our villeins. Her dislike for Fitzralph as villein-bullier was intense, and his ears must have burned painfully on those occasions when she spoke of him. Sister Harley was developing most satisfactorily ...

It seemed I had hardly dropped off when there came a noisy pounding on the door to my quarters. I heard Mellie shout, "Yes, yes, I'm coming!" as she rose from her pallet, and I began to lever my old bones out of my too-soft bed. When Mellie opened the door there was an excited gabble of voices — some of them male, which boded ill. I draped my overdress about myself like a toga and tottered out to see what was the matter.

"... Lady Bertille!" I recognized the speaker as Papion, our Porter, keeper of the main gate. "She's been attacked; she's hurt!"

"Where is she?" I asked, trying to see who else was there by the dim light of the single-wick cresset that burns beside the fireplace all night.

"Ma-*dame!*" trilled Mellie. "You are *not* Properly Dressed! There are *men* present!"

"If the men will turn their backs, you can dress me!" I replied crossly. "Now, what has happened to Lady Bertille?"

Mellie quickly lit two fat candles from the cresset and suddenly I could see three of them just inside the door: Elizabeth Freemantle, Austin, and Papion. All had politely turned their backs. It was Elizabeth who spoke. "Madame, Lady Bertille has come on foot and alone to our gate." This was in itself an extraordinary thing. "She has been severely beaten and — and raped."

"*Raped!* Who has done this thing to her?"

"My lady, she will not say," replied Austin.

"Well, bring her to our infirmary. Couldn't her own people protect her?" My voice became muffled as Mellie dropped a fresh overdress over my head. "Why has she not sent for her own doctor? Why has she come here?"

Elizabeth turned around, her face streaming tears. "My lady, she has come here for *Sanctuary!*"

Sanctuary! That meant she thought the man was still after her. "Papion!" I cried. "Why have you left the gate? Return at once! And set watches on the bell tower and atop the granary! A great lady is in peril of her life! Away with you!" Papion, at eighteen, was a good man, but perhaps a little young for his responsibility. He ducked out the door hastily.

Mellie had dragged my great carved chair out from behind my work table and began to work my feet into the soft boots we wore for night offices.

"Elizabeth," I said, "bring Lady Bertille into the church. Stay with her, try to calm her if she's frightened. Say I will be there soon. Send someone to awaken Sister Mary so she can bring bandages, medicines and bedding to the church. Quickly, go now!"

"Yes Madame," she said and vanished down the passageway that leads out of the cloister with a clatter of the pattens she wore against the mud left by yesterday's rain.

"Austin, you awaken Father Hugh, explain what has happened and ask him to come at once to the church. Then check to make sure Papion has made good arrangements. Tell him to send Bodrey with a message if anything happens."

"Yes, m'lady. I'll watch a while on the gate with him."

"Good man. Thank you. Now go!"

Mellie had begun to fuss over my veil, but I stood and pulled away from her. "Enough!" I said; cold fear made me snap. "I am as well dressed as ever I was for the middle of the night!"

The only man who would want or dare to attack Lady Bertille, surely, was Sir Ranulf. He would never dare attack her at Dowse, which had men at arms and numerous servants; no, he was doubtless at Chimneys, as Sister Mildred said. This could only mean one thing.

I went quickly to the church, and arrived at the same time as Lady Bertille. Walter Avenger, our chief stableman, was carrying her, and she was weeping with harsh, ragged sobs. He laid her gently at the foot of the altar and went out silently. I went at once to her.

"What were you doing at *Chimneys?*" I demanded.

She turned to me, her face bruised and swollen; I was horrified to see her beauty so marred. "Dust," she said, choking back sobs.

"What?" I said blankly.

"Walls broken down to make new rooms. Lots of dust. Could not stop sneezing — ridiculous. Rode to Chimneys at sunset to spend night."

She began to weep again, and I tried to comfort her, and thought about how stupidly we order our lives.

Sister Mary arrived with Sister Emma, laden with several pallets, clean bed linen, bandages, warm water, ointment and poppy drink. We gently removed most of Lady Bertillon' s clothing and were saddened to find the marks of a severe beating. We were cleaning and dressing her wounds when Father Hugh came in all in a rush, his monk's robe awry.

I have often wondered about our old priest. He had seen much in his seventy-three years, yet his heart remained innocent as a dove's. I don't think he saw that Bertille was nearly naked, only that she was in great pain and distress, for he came at once to kneel beside her. Her face was so bruised he could not kiss her, and broken fingers prevented him from holding her hand; yet his face reflected none of the dismay he must have felt, only gentle greeting and concern.

"I seek to dwell in the house of the Lord," she murmured when she saw him.

"For in the day of trouble He will keep me safe in His shelter; He shall hide me in the secrecy of His dwelling," Father Hugh replied in kind. "A wicked man has done this to you."

"Nine wicked men; I counted," she whispered. "The tenth was too drunk."

"But chief among them was the wolf's head," said Father Hugh.

"I did not tell you that," she objected feebly.

"No, but I know it nevertheless," said Father Hugh.

She hesitated. "Yes," she assented.

He stood and removed the two lit candles from the altar and set them near her head on either side and began to rummage in the small, black wooden chest he had brought with him. "Now, brave lady, have you anything to get off your chest?" he asked conversationally, as he kissed his purple stole and draped it around his neck.[xxxvi]

"*I?*" she replied, echoing faintly his almost-bantering tone.

"Yes, like the dismissal of your lady-in-waiting Sabina, and sending her home with a sharp note because she told you tawny velvet made your skin look a funny color." Although he still smiled, Father Hugh's tone was firm.

Well! I thought. What an extraordinary way to begin the Sacrament of Penance! (And where, I wondered, did he learn *that?*) I quickly bade Elizabeth and Sisters Mary and Emma come with me to the back of the church, where we stayed until Father Hugh signaled us to return. Bertille was calm, and she had that newly-washed look of the freshly shriven. Father Hugh then went on with the Sacrament of Extreme Unction, anointing her eyelids, ears, nostrils, mouth, hands and feet with holy oil, praying that the Lord would forgive her any sins committed through the use of these members. He cleaned the oil from his fingers with a small wad of bread, which he put aside to be burned later. Then he changed his purple stole for a white one, removed a white wafer from a silver box in the chest, and after some prayers placed it carefully on her tongue. "Receive, sister, the Viaticum of the Body of our Lord, Jesus Christ," he said.

Then he rather hastily packed his little chest and left without further conversation, like a man late for an appointment. I remember thinking that he was undoubtedly a holy man, but getting rather old and peculiar.

The midnight bell rang then, a call to Matins. Bertille watched quietly as my ladies filed in and hasty explanations were passed around. She joined in the Psalms of the long night-time offices, and refused the poppy drink I offered her afterward, saying she wanted to talk, if I would stay with her. So I sent my ladies back to bed and sat on a cushion on the long step across the edge of the Sanctuary. I was dismayed all over again at the state of her face and hands.

"You are getting full of worldly vanity, Margaret," she said through puffy lips, noting my left thumb with one eye — the other being swollen shut. "I thought only men were proud enough to carry about so weighty a piece of gold." Her ruined face belied the healthy spirit within — she was teasing to comfort *me*.

I glanced down at the ring. "I put the tiresome thing on and it won't come off," I mock-grumbled. "Richard of Gloucester begged shelter of us from the rain yestereve, and gave us this ring in payment."

"The King's brother? *That* Richard?"

"Yes, the frail-looking one who wins battles. That one."

"I hear he lives in Warwick's pocket," she gossiped with a ghost of her old smile.

"Poor Warwick," I said in my best dry tone.

"I remember when I was afraid of you, Margaret."

"Of *me?*"

"When I first came to Dowse Manor I was only fifteen years old and newly wed. I was soon told stories about this strict abbess who would not allow even the most noble of her nuns the ordinary decent things their sisters in the world had. I was afraid you'd rebuke me for living a life of ease, and see by my face I enjoyed the marital state all too well." Again the smile flickered.

"You haven't had an easy life after all, have you?" I asked. "Your son has died, Sir John is away a great deal, and you have more on your shoulders than I, for your lands are greater."

"And now *this,*" she groaned, and began to cry. "Oh, Margaret, he was so cruel and hard — and all the while *laughing!* Nothing can touch him, *nothing!* He is adamantine wickedness!"

"Nay, love, one day the sheriff will come for him, and for all his tongue may go on wheels, yet he'll make a pudding for crows![xxxvii] Meanwhile his doings with you are over. You are safe here, within three encircling walls, and beside the very altar of a church consecrated these two hundred years." I stopped to see if she would rise to my bait.

The weeping slowed. "*Two* hundred? But you tell the chance pilgrim this abbey was founded by Alfred the Great — *six* hundred years ago!"

"*I?* You must be thinking of Sister Mary or Sister Alys. Oh, yes, common talk would have it that we are that old, but I am quite sure we are barely from the time of Edward the Confessor.[xxxviii] And, anyway, this present church was built with funds given to us by Eleanor of Castile, and she died in 1290!"

Lady Bertille looked around the dimly-lit church as if seeing it for the first time. "Is that the sort of thing you learn poring over those musty old parchments of yours?"

"You speak too lightly of my favorite amusement. Once my Latin sharpened up, I have found it a fascinating way to spend a rainy afternoon. Do you know I once found a deed for two houses plugging a gap between wall and window frame? And I have found important documents hidden among old bills of sale and among testy letters from some long-dead bishop. It is like finding pearls in the grass; one simply cannot stop looking for just one more."[xxxix]

She tried to laugh and moaned. "I wish I had a deed to convince Sir Ranulf he has no claim to Chimneys!"

Staring at her, I said, "But you *do* — oh, Bertille, you *must!* Why, I have a duly sworn *copy* of it! I can even remember what it says: Your husband's grandfather, Sir Edward (the one whose effigy is over there in the corner, on his tomb) bought it from Sir Walter Sinclare. Sinclare is the name of a line of cousins to the Fitzralphs. Sir Walter Sinclare was undoubtedly a spendthrift, for he sold Sir Edward three parcels of land about the same time all for less than their worth."

Bertille's one open eye stared back at me, large with astonishment. "*You* have a copy of the deed?"

Her long pale hair hung motionless about her bruised face.

"Why — yes! You could not find the deed? Why didn't you ask *me?* Bertille, you know abbeys often hold valuables in safe deposit for people — including deeds! Why I have copies of twenty and more de Cynegil transactions." I looked away from that awful eye. "I am surprised," I said as mildly as I could, "that Sir John did not advise you to ask me."

"I didn't want to worry him with my troubles when he was fighting," she whispered. "He doesn't know about this trouble with Sir Ranulf."

Then she begged, "Oh, Margaret, tell me it doesn't make any difference, that Fitzralph would have come even if I had the deed!"

I hesitated, then told the truth. "He would have come anyway, because Sir John is away — but perhaps not so boldly or so soon. And I'm sure he didn't *plan* to surprise you at Chimneys."

"No," she said in a small, tired voice, "but he was very pleased to see me. I think I will have that poppy stuff now." So I helped her drink it and willingly stayed with her until she fell asleep; then blessed her for the right singular well-beloved lady she was to me, and went to weep myself asleep.

I'm sure Adonai must have made her tentative "ting-ting" before beginning her bronze shout. But by the time I was awake enough to really hear, she was already drawing out her note in that distorted way that means she is nearly standing on her head at the end of each swing — her cry of alarm.[xl]

Mellie came quickly to help me dress again. My heart was a stone within my breast. "What hour must it be?" she wondered anxiously.

"Less than an hour to dawn, I think," I replied. "We will look at Lady Bertille first."

But my friend was safely deep in drugged sleep, oblivious to the clamor of the bell. I went next to the dorter, to find my nuns had already dressed and gone away; so we hurried as fast as my legs would allow down the stairs to my quarters, through, and out the door to the short passageway to the inner courtyard. There we found my ladies and the servants who live in the cloister and inner courtyard clustered around the big wooden gate leading to the outer court. Several carried torches, which gave a dim orange light to the scene. "Hurry!" called someone as Simon Hine struggled with the heavy bar of the gate, and we hastened across to join them.

"What's amiss?" I called.

"Wool barn's afire, m'lady!" called Agnes de Ran, our chief cook, stepping out from the rest, a torch in her hand, bending her short, plump body in a bow.

The gate began to swing towards us, bringing with it a faint smell of smoke and a glimmer of dark flame at the far end of the outer court. Mellie and I joined the end of the procession out the gate. I was hoping we could save not only the wool stored in the barn but perhaps some of the looms, dye vats, and other paraphernalia. It was very dark at the back of the crowd, and I dropped well back so as not to step on anyone's hem.

Then a powerful blow knocked me down, and there were torches around me. I looked up indignantly and saw a man with a sword standing over me. He moved as if to use his weapon; I threw my left arm up to save myself, and the big golden ring caught the light of the torches. "*Hold!*" came a sharp command, and another man came quickly forward to grab at the ring. Then he saw the white boar on it and paused. He was roughly dressed and wore a hood pulled well forward over his head, but his bearing was noble and his hand grasping mine was beautifully gloved.

"Gloucester!" he muttered. "This one cannot be bought or frightened!" (He was not speaking of me; I was terrified.) He flung my hand down. "Leave be!" We've other fish to fry!" As they hurried towards the Priest's Gate leading to the church, I heard him reassure his eight or nine henchmen, "It's all right! The old bat is half blind!" Which was true enough — but I was far from deaf. And I had no trouble identifying that particular voice as Fitzralph's.

They quickly formed a sort of tumbler's tower before the Priest's Gate and tossed the highest man over the wall, so he could open it for them. When he did, I could see by the flaring light of their torches a small figure in their way. It was old Father Hugh, late answering the alarm because he had put on his armor. He was staggering slightly under the weight of his most enormous quarterstaff. I was surprised to see Fitzralph and his men hesitate. Father Hugh was but one little old man against their nine or ten and even his air of indomitable righteousness could hardly have counted for much against such odds.

Fitzralph gestured and said something and most of his men ran towards the church, leaving two behind, one with a torch. Fitzralph drew his sword and Father Hugh raised his quarterstaff.

Again Sir Ranulf hesitated. He swung his sword tentatively and Father Hugh blocked it easily and returned to his original pose. Fitzralph tested again, with more force, and then feinted at the priest's left ear and when the long staff shifted to parry swiftly altered his aim and dealt a blow of sickening force down and deep into Father Hugh's right shoulder, seeming to cleave him to the breastbone, armor and all.

Fitzralph said something and his two men laughed, and they ran for the church. I was left in near darkness. The church bell took on a flattened note. I became aware that my right arm was paining me very sharply. There was shouting from the direction of my wool barn, now burning briskly. My priest lay ominously still where he had fallen.

And even now Lady Bertille, helplessly asleep, was being murdered by that bloody man, Fitzralph. The blessed order of my Abbey was in a shambles and it was *his* doing — I was suddenly full of a fury that was almost exhilarating. I began to struggle against my entangling garb and then to weep because I could not stand and strike him down.

In a little while they came streaming back. One, at least, was a little worried about their deeds. "By these ten bones," he said, flinging out his hand, "I like this not! Sacrilege, just to bake that bitch's bread!"[xli]

"Who cares what you think, buzzard!" hissed his companion. "Just do as Sir Ranulf says, and we'll be all right." They slipped into the outer court and were gone.

I rose onto my knees and tried to shout to those around the blazing barn to intercept Fitzralph, but my voice was a croak and I could not raise the hue and cry.

But Mellie could. She scuttled from behind the commonfolk guest-house and raced out the gate shouting, "*Help! Murder! Stop them!*" After several repeats, the cry was taken up and the chase begun.

Mellie returned to me. "Are you all right, my lady?" she asked, helping me to my feet.

"I am quite shaken, and my right arm is either very badly sprained or broken. Mellie, quickly, fetch a light and some sheets; Father Hugh and Lady Bertille are dead, I think."

"Your arm — *broken?* Oh, m'lady! I will take you to your bed! We must send at once for a doctor!"

I turned in icy fury on her. "For once you will do *as* I say *when* I say, without argument! Now go at once for a lamp and sheets!" She gaped wordlessly, and then hurried away. I had never used that tone of voice to her before.

But I could not wait for her return. I groped my way in the semi-darkness to kneel beside Father Hugh. "*In manus, tuas, Domine, commendo spiritum eum,*"[xlii] I murmured. "Silly old man!" I tried to arrange his limbs decently — he had fallen all in a heap — but the terribleness of his wound, and the darkness, and my useless arm, and the awkwardness of his armor, and the dreadful *stickiness* of everything, made a nightmare of my attempts.

When I saw Mellie returning with the lamp and sheets I called out to her, "No, no! Don't come near! I will come to you!"

As I approached, she looked at me so fearfully that I glanced down at myself. I was smeared and bedabbled with blood. "*His,* Mellie, *his!* Father Hugh's!" And I took a sheet from her and covered the little form.

Sister Mildred came through the open gate, calling for me. When I answered, she said, "Oh, thank God! I thought you were killed!" She exclaimed breathlessly over my appearance and injury and, between exclamations, explained that the hue and cry after the murderers had to be spread outside the Abbey — all the men on watch had deserted their posts to fight the fire, and so Fitzralph and his henchmen had gotten away.

"Will God not send me to be better served than *this?!*" I raged, and turned to hobble to the church, Mellie and Sister Mildred trailing in my wake.

I sent Sister Mildred up to order the bell stopped, and she and Father Clement — he exhausted and dizzy — joined me by the Sanctuary where Lady Bertille lay. She appeared to be in the abandon of sleep, but there was a small red stain in her side around a rent in the pale green garment we had dressed her in earlier. "It doesn't look big enough to have let her soul escape, does it?" I said sadly as Sister Mildred and I floated the sheet over her.

"No, my lady," murmured Father Clement, looking at my own bloody gown fearfully.

"Look, my lady!" called Mellie. "They have attacked Sir Edward! His nose is clean gone!" It did indeed look as if someone had hacked at the marble effigy with a blade, and the high, hooked nose that was a de Cynegil family trait was broken off.

"We can look for it in the daylight," I said. "Mellie, come help me clean myself, and change; then bring a stool for me to the wool barn, for I will see this thing through."

"The church is desecrated," pronounced Father Clement in awful tones, but as if just realizing it. "We will have to send for the bishop." He staggered to the choir stalls and sat down heavily — he was rather frail, although not above forty years old.

He was right: Willful murder in a consecrated church made it unfit for use until a bishop performed a ceremony called reconciliation. "Bishop Morys is at Banbury," I said. "We can send for him at first light. Meanwhile I will go watch my barn burn. Father Clement, I will send Tom Dryver and Peter Ploughmaystre to help you move Lady Bertille's body to — to where?"

"Might I suggest the calefactory, Madame?" offered Sister Mildred meekly. "We do not need a warming room during the summer."

"Thank you, Sister. And, Father Clement, Father Hugh's body will be brought to the calefactory as well." He looked horrified and crossed himself. "He was cut down by the same as did this. You will clear the altar, put out the lights and lock the doors. Then you will lead Tom and Peter in prayers for our dead. Is that clear?"

"Quite," he said faintly. He looked frightened and I had no time for frightened men. I fled before his terror could infect me.

With dawn of that dreadful Friday morning, a mist began rising that mixed with the smoke of the dying fire. It made our eyes run and set us coughing. As word of the murders spread, there was weeping. But I looked at each pair of red eyes and wondered: was it bereavement or smoke that made the tears flow? For anger had frozen my heart, and left it a heavy weight within my breast.

When the fire was safely out, Austin came to me and begged to be allowed to bind my broken arm to a stick, which would prevent further injury to the flesh of my arm. He was careful, but his attentions only increased the pain.

I declared the service of Prime delayed for one hour, then bade Sister Harley accompany me to my quarters.

There, to my dictation, she wrote a hasty letter to Bishop Morys in which I gave a brief account of the desecration and begged him to come reconcile our church as soon as humanly possible. I put my personal seal on it, and the Deer Abbey seal, and she addressed it. "Which is faster, the gray or the dun?" I asked her. (I had not ridden for the last year or so because of the infirmity of my limbs.)

"The gray, my lady," she replied. "Bodrey to ride?" She was ever quick to catch my thought unspoken.

"Yes, he is small and a good horseman. Take this letter to him and give him enough money to hire a nag to come home on if he wears out the gray — but he is not to kill the gray in his haste! He should give this into the hand of Bishop Morys himself. If the bishop is not at Banbury, he is to ride to wherever he is; he is not to return until the message is safely delivered."

"Yes, my lady," said Sister Harley and departed at once but without rushing. Sister Harley never rushed, a trait I found very restful.

Prime was held in the Chapter House, and a meeting was called after Prime in the great hall of our guest-house. As I walked through the crowd toward the carved chair placed for me on the dais, I noted that not only every servant and villein from within the Abbey was present, but also a crowd of villeins from Deerfield (some of them not even Abbey villeins), along with a sprinkling of men in de Cynegil livery. All had answered our alarm and helped to fight the fire. Those nearest bowed to me politely or humbly. The noisy room reeked of smoke and sweat.

On orders from Sister Mildred, half a dozen children were passing among them with loaves of bread and pitchers of ale, so the people could refresh themselves.

And there in the midst of them stood Lady Angharad, Lady Bertille's daughter, in an immaculate bagged-sleeve houppeland of light blue and dark green. She bent one knee, then raised her pale face with its large, clear gray eyes to me. Her black hair was neatly hidden under a hood, and she appeared utterly composed.

"What is it you want, child?" I asked (though she was no longer a child, being nearly seventeen).

"To ask you privily one question."

I considered her a moment, then consented and let her walk beside me to a place behind my chair, which was large enough to serve as a confessional. "Have you come to take your mother home?" I asked gently.

"Huddson will make the arrangements. After I saw her I couldn't — I couldn't — that is *not* my mother!" She began to tremble violently. I turned and saw Mellie, standing a little out of conversational range. "Wine, Mellie, quickly!" I called. She swiftly produced a cup, and Angharad took a single deep draught. What fool, I thought, had drawn back that sheet for Angharad?

"My lady," I said, "that is indeed your mother. I talked with her a long while last night, and she was brave and of good cheer, as only someone of her breeding and backbone could have been."

But Angharad was not listening. "I will ask my question now," she said. "Who did this to her?" Her tone was quiet and even.

I studied her smooth countenance carefully and realized it was a mask for a rage as bitter as mine. I thought also of how she was the sole surviving child of Lady Bertille and Sir John, and until Sir John came home or named a guardian, had at her command a considerable force of armed men. Surely among them there was one she could trust with an ugly task. I did not think Sir Ranulf's immunity broken. Angharad had to strike at him, or his next target might be her. Her blood must not be allowed to cool.

Therefore I set aside the gentle words I would have spoken to her and said, "I did not see the face of the man — " She groaned. "— but I recognized his voice and his walk." I drew her with my eyes and aimed the arrow of her fury deliberately. "Sir Ranulf Fitzralph murdered your mother."

She sucked a hissing breath through her teeth, pressed the cup into my hands and left the room at a walk so brisk the white linen of her underdress flashed at her heels. And when I looked down at the bowl of the goblet I saw that her small hands had bent it into a crooked oval.

I sent Sisters Emma and Alison to speak with Huddson about taking Lady Bertille's corpse to the family chapel at Dowse.

Then I took my seat and the meeting began. My ladies arranged themselves on stools on either side of my chair. I announced formally the deaths of Lady Bertille and Father Hugh and said that Father Hugh would be buried in our church as soon as it was cleansed by Bishop Morys, who had been sent for. The church was desecrated, I said, when Sir Ranulf Fitzralph and his men murdered Lady Bertille as she lay in Sanctuary. The weight in my chest swelled as if to choke me as I spoke.

There was a lengthy murmuring as the explanation of Lady Bertille's seeking Sanctuary was given round, along with her condition on arrival.

As I waited for the murmurs to cease, I noticed several of the non-Abbey villeins slipping towards the door. Most seemed to have put on the innocent look that means they are up to something, but that was no business of mine. I watched them go thinking it was as well, as I would hold inquest into this incident, making a Manor Court of the meeting, and my authority could not reach to them.

"*Now,*" I said sternly, searching the nervous faces of my people, "*who let Sir Ranulf in?*"

Papion appeared, to kneel at my feet. "I am in your mercy, Madame!" he said. The left side of his head was a bruised and bloody mess. When he saw the expression on my face, he fell prostrate.

"Up, fellow! On your knees! Let me hear your story!" Obediently, he pushed himself up. "M'lady, it was after three o' th' clock," he began, his voice shaky, dragging a filthy sleeve across a begrimed forehead. "I was at my post, when I heard a woman knocking at the gate and crying to be let in. I called out who was it, and she said she was Bessie Sayer, servant to Lady Bertille, and she was beaten half to death and some men were after her to finish her off. So I opened the gate and something crashed on my head and next thing I knew old Gyb from the village was shaking me."

"Where is Bessie Sayer?"

"Don't know m'lady. Run away, maybe."

Austin came forward at that. "No, she isn't, Madame. She lies dead in Shearing Meadow, across from the gate. She looks beaten, but not badly — but her throat's been cut."

Another corpse! Was there no end to this bloody business! "Hodge," I called, catching our reeve's eye, "please see if you can catch Huddson and let him know Lady Bertille's servant lies dead in Shearing Meadow, so he can take her as well."

"Ye'm," replied the faithful Hodge, and departed.

Papion reminded me he was still in my mercy by falling on his face again. I let him stay there. "Austin, what do you think? They brought the Sayer woman to the gate and made her ask for entry?"

"Yes, Madame, and this fool did not think to climb to an upper floor and look out. Those men had at least one torch with them, to light the others off once inside. If he'd looked, he'd have seen the torch, I think."

"Papion, I will delay any action against you until I have consulted in Chapter with my ladies. You will return to your post at the gate." Our Holy Rule commands us to select a "wise old man" as Porter, and by not obeying we had brought great damage on ourselves. Papion rose slowly and exited with a sad and thoughtful face.

"Now, who first saw the fire?" I asked.

"I did, m'lady." It was Tiff Tybalt, one of our villeins, noted for his ability to keep later, longer wakes than any other villein.[xliii] He was about forty-five, tall for a villein, very thin, with a large nose. "Pap sent me to watch on th' granary roof, and about halfway twixt Matins and Prime I saw a man with a firebrand run along th'wool-barn, up one side and down t'other, touching off thatch. 'Who dares t'do such a thing?' I thought. I reckon now that devil Sir Ranulf sent him to draw us away from cloister."

"Could you see who it was?"

"No'm. I shouted 'Fire! Fire in th' wool barn!' as loud as I could, and ran down the steps to see if I could catch him — and by God I *did!*" he growled with a savage smile. "He ran behind the great barn, and you know you can't get through there — the buttress on th' far end touches th' wall!" He paused to savor the recollection, as the listeners waited breathlessly for him to continue.

"Like a rat, he was: trapped," said Tiff. "I fetched out my old friend here —" he tapped the long knife he always wore on his belt — "and went to speak o' Lydford Law with him. He'd dropped his brand and it was dark as —" Tiff caught himself and glanced hastily at me "— dark as the inside of a cow, and he nearly sneaked by me. I grabbed him and we tussled a bit, then I stuck him —" he made two swift, short arcs with his fist, ugly and graphic — "and he went down like he was poleaxed. Never made a sound!" He stopped to rake in the sighs and murmurs of admiration.

"Where is he? Where did you put him?"

"Put him? M'lady, why put him anyplace? Roll him into a ditch and call him buried, when you've a spare moment, for he lies dead as Pontius Pilate right where he fell."[xliv] This commentary passed for both wit and wisdom in the mood of that gathering.

I spoke then of events in the inner courtyard, of how I recognized Sir Ranulf and how Richard Gloucester's ring saved my life (for which he was roundly cheered when I held up my still-imprisoned thumb). I blamed myself for not ordering watches set at the inner gate, where they would have seen Sir

Ranulf waiting on its opening. (Richard was right; we trusted too much to our strong walls.) I spoke bitterly of Father Hugh's death, for the reason they came was to kill Lady Bertille.

Father Hugh would remain in the calefactory (which could not warm my priest to life again!) until our church was reconciled by Bishop Morys and we could have his funeral and burial. "Sisters Alison and Emma will relieve Father Clement, Tom Dryver and Peter Ploughmaystre at the dead watch after dinner."

I looked around the room. "Is there anything else to be discussed?" Gyb Cotter was surreptitiously stuffing half a loaf of bread into his tunic, but he was desperately poor and I said nothing.

One of the children who had been dispensing ale stood forward. She had an impenetrable tangle of black hair and hardly any clothing and, looking shy, muttered something almost inaudible. "What is it, child?" I asked sharply.

"She says the bell is broken, my lady," said Austin, who was standing near her. "Your indulgence a moment." He stooped and held a brief conversation with her, then addressed me again. "She is Cissy Dryver, and went a while ago to take her father some ale in the warming room, and while there Father Clement told her the bell cracked when it was being rung last night."

"I *did* hear it change note after I was attacked," I said thoughtfully. "I think it was before Sir Ranulf went into the church. Thank you, child; you did well to bring us this news." If the bell was only cracked, it might be repaired; Austin said he would investigate.

"Is there anything else?"

There was a struggle near the back of the room, then old Jack Garth, our head gardener and beekeeper, was thrust forward to the accompaniment of giggles and orders to "tell her!"

Jack stopped grinning when he saw my face and cleared his throat noisily several times. "M'lady, there's a monsterous great swan in th' orchard near warming room, a vile, ill-tempered beast I can't drive away, for it hisses and threatens t' break th' arm of anyone tries to come near. I saw it when I went to check th' hives after we got th' barn fire out this mornin'. Twasn't there yestereve."

"Thank you, Jack. Is there anything *else?*" There wasn't. I said we would meet in our Chapter House for the prayers of our office until our church was reconciled, and that the prayers would commence at None. Then I dismissed the meeting.

Most of our people went to bed, while others stood watch, and Sisters Harley and Mildred came with me to my quarters to take dictation. "Tell the cooks we will eat dinner after None," I said to Sister Clara and shut the door firmly upon my chamber. I had to open it a short while later to eject Mellie, who kept fussing at me to go to bed. I was far too busy to take to my bed, and the pain in my arm would have kept me from sleep at any rate.

I dictated a letter first to the King, "the mighty and most noble King Edward," explaining what had befallen us and asking for his justice as King and aid as overlord of the Abbey.

Then we wrote to the Duke of Gloucester, the "right high and mighty Richard," explaining we had a "singular confidence in your noble lordship's good grace afore any others," and, reminding him of the promise he made during his visit, asking him to intercede for us before the King before we were all killed in our beds.[xlv]

We wrote John Freemantle, explaining what had transpired, saying it was not necessary that he should come home, that his wife and children were well, and that we were writing because I sought to have him armed with the truth — bad as it was — rather than dealing blindly with rumors I was sure were coming his way.

With great care and a good deal of discussion we composed a letter to Sir John telling of the death of his wife. I described her as brave and of good cheer up to the last moment I saw her, and noted she had received the last sacraments of the Church and so no doubt had already been escorted to a comfortable place in Abraham's bosom,[xlvi] "for I doubt a lady so kind and good as your wife would spend even an instant in Purgatory," adding to Sister Harley in an aside, "particularly in light of the suffering she endured before her death."

We were working on a short letter to Doctor John le Spitelman at Oxford when Elizabeth knocked and opened my door and, without a word, showed in Lady Angharad. She was still in her houppeland, which looked as if it had been dragged through thorn bushes. Her hood had been pulled back and her fine black hair was flying loose. She was very white, with two bright patches on her cheeks, and her hands displayed a fine tremor. She curtsied very deeply and barely regained her feet.

"I have been hunting, Lady Margaret," she said in a high, strained voice. "Isn't that a fine way to mourn one's mother?"

"Did you catch anything?" I asked inanely.

"Oh *yes!* Yes I did!" She clasped her hands to her stomach and Elizabeth took her arm as she was about to fall. We placed her in my chair and I gave her a goblet with a small dose of Elizabeth of Hungary's remarkable medicine, for that and water were the only drinkables we had at hand — and she needed more than water. She choked over it but it faded the red patches a bit and brought some color to her lips.

When she could speak she said, "My liam dogs have killed Sir Ranulf and they are fighting over his umbles this minute!"[xlvii] And I dropped the cup I had taken from her hand.

"My lady, what have you done?" asked Sister Mildred sharply.

"Tolly Bond, our reeve, met me at our gate when I got home. He said Fitzralph's villeins heard from you who killed Father Hugh and my mother, and they had risen and fired their master's house. But Sir Ranulf had escaped into Wychwood on foot." She looked up at me calmly. "He always gets away, you know. The bailiff, the jury, the enraged father, the desperate villein, the pain-maddened horse, the burning building — all, *all* strike in vain at him!"

"Hush, my lady, hush!" I said. "What happened?"

"I thought about what he had done to my lady mother and what —" She closed her eyes and said in an oddly conversational tone, "He has always been very nice to me, especially since my brother died last year." Then, "I asked myself, how would my father handle this? I knew I had to act promptly. If Sir Ranulf returned, what unspeakable things would he do to the villeins who burned his house? I had a responsibility. He was a wolf's head, and it is the lord's duty to protect his people from wolves."

"How did you catch him?" I asked.

She almost laughed. "It was too easy! My dogs are often used to chase thieves or runaway villeins. Our houndsman — you know him, Elizabeth, he's Wat Berner —he helped the dogs find the trail where Fitzralph entered Wychwood, and we two just followed. He showed no skill, no doubling on his trail or running upstream to lose his scent. He didn't even climb a tree. Ah, they howled and barked after him, and in less than an hour I saw him lurking in the holly." She licked her nether lip. Her light gray eyes did not see any of us. "I — I told Wat to loose the dogs. They were about to choke on their collars in their excitement. He laughed — he laughed — and loosed them with a shout, and they scrambled for a chance at their quarry.

"He screamed, once. We waited a Paternoster while — I said it very slowly, to be sure — and came to see if he was dead."

"Was he?" I could not seem to stop asking foolish questions. "Oh, yes, he was quite truly and completely dead." She swallowed, and again in that odd tone, said, "I wonder, should I go and cut off his head and send it to the King for the bounty?" And she began at last to weep most bitterly.

I touched her shoulder and she grasped my hand and pressed it to her cheek while I made soothing, ineffectual noises. I heard Sister Harley take Sister Mildred to the door and, after some instructions, send her out. I could not think what to say to this demolished Angharad. She was always so brave and high-spirited. I had aimed her at Sir Ranulf — and the sweet vengeance I sought was ashes in my mouth. Elizabeth began to help me calm her. "There, there, sweetling."

"Every time I close my eyes," sobbed Angharad, "I see him on the ground before me. *What* am I to do?"

"*Nothing!*" said Sister Harley suddenly from across the room. "My lady, I could cudgel my brains and have no answer for you. We are sickened by what happened to Sir Ranulf — but if it were not done, the whole shire would have *strangled* on his vengeance!"

I asked, my voice reflecting my pain and guilt, "Surely you could have sent another to do the deed?"

"What, burden another's soul with a murder to benefit one's self? I think *not!*" said Elizabeth warmly, patting Angharad. "I admit *I* would have talked some sturdy rogue into doing the deed — but *I* am not of noble blood!" At that quick reply some of the bitterness seemed to go from Angharad's tears.

"Come, my lady," I said gently to her. "You may stay awhile in our guest-house, and Elizabeth will stay with you until you are more yourself. We have delayed dinner until None; will you join us?"

"Thank you, no. But I *will* stay with Elizabeth. You are kind to give me her company." She stood clumsily, and Elizabeth supported her.

"I will send for you at Vespers," I said.

"I am very sorry, my lady," she replied faintly, "but prayers stick in my throat now even as food does." So I sent her away with my blessing, poor lady.

After the two were gone, Sister Harley said, "I told Sister Mildred to tell Austin what had happened to Sir Ranulf, and for him to arrange to gather the, er, remains in a decent shroud and bury them outside the cemetery wall in Deerfield, after telling Father Christopher of it. And to kill the dogs."

"That was well and timely done, Sister. Thank you." My voice was thick.

"Yes, but *what* will we tell the King's men when they come?"

I said tiredly, "We will tell them the truth! — Except for Lady Angharad's role, maybe," I amended after an instant's thought. "Someone should go see Wat Berner, to see what sort of man he is, and what he has said to anyone of this, and how loyal to Lady Angharad he may be." I sought my chair blindly. "Oh, Bertille, what have I done to your daughter?"

I decided to lie down for a while. Mellie came to me and partly undressed me, and I lay back on the soft featherbed. But the pain in my arm — or was it remorse? — made me tremble. My conscience spoke mercilessly to me until I groaned, "Oh, God, be merciful to me, a sinner!"

After a while, Sister Harley was sent for; she read to me from our copy of an alliterative Morte d'Arthur as a distraction. Mellie tried to encourage my attention. "'Swept him down with his swift sword!'" she repeated approvingly.

There was a soft knock and Mellie opened my door to Elizabeth. "What is it? I cried, sitting up when I heard her voice. "Has something happened to Angharad?"

"No, no, my lady. She is sleeping soundly. I was restless and afraid I would disturb her, so I took a walk around the outer court." Elizabeth came around the screen that guards my bed. "And I met a man who can set your arm!"

"We are sending for Dr. Spitelman, who can be here day after tomorrow," said Sister Harley coolly.

"But this man says broken arms should be set as quickly as possible. And Dr. Spitelman may check it for wrongness, if you wish, when he comes."

"Who is he?" I asked, for I knew of no doctor in our neighborhood.

"He is a chirurgeon. He served in the King's army and knows a great deal about broken bones, having set many hundreds, he says."

"Is he a guest here?" Sister Harley was not very impressed. A chirurgeon was a long way from a doctor. "What is his name?"

"Lucas Barber. And he is not a guest, he —" she hesitated and drew a deep breath. "He is the one-legged beggar who often sits by our gate."

Sister Harley and Mellie began to laugh. "That ragamuffin!" squeaked Mellie.

I saw Elizabeth was in earnest. "Be silent!" I ordered the other two. I had enough experience with broken bones to know that if they were set, the pain diminished greatly.

Elizabeth flashed me a grateful look and said, "I have spoken often with him. His leg was blown away when a bombard blew up because the gunpowder was too strong.[xlviii] His skills remain in his hands. Truly, his voice and manners show him to be a man of decent breeding and good mind!"

"Well, I suppose a beggar may be an honest man. Surely it will do no harm to speak to him. Where is he?"

"In the commonfolk lodge. Tiff will help him wash the dust of the road from his person."

"Sister Harley, as Hosteler you will go greet him courteously and offer him a change of clothing. And have Sister Mary consult with him about what he will need to properly set my arm, in case he proves himself. Then bring him here." She assented with becoming meekness.

In a little while the cloister bell rang and Sister Harley returned with Elizabeth, and behind them Sister Mary (carrying bandages and splints), followed by a sturdy-looking sunburned man with bright brown hair and light blue eyes. He was wearing a smokey-blue houppeland and walking with the aid of a crudely-made crutch. His speech betrayed his London origins, but he was no cockney. I may have recognized him for a beggar I had sometimes seen, but he assumed an air of authority so naturally that I immediately forgot the recognition.

He ordered a stool pulled up and had me sit in my chair behind the work table, with my arm resting on it. "We will remove the present bandage," he said, and did so very gently. The arm was swollen and purple. "Good," he said, "the bone has not pierced the skin." His strong and knowing fingers began to manipulate my forearm and I instantly cried out. "Yes, shout all you like, my lady," he said cheerfully, "this is very painful. Just don't jostle the arm. Ah, only one of the forearm bones is broken."

He began a blood-curdling description of a broken hip he once set by means of a machine with a turnscrew and suddenly, as with a little click, the bone ends met and matched. "There!" he said. "Now the splints and bandages. I am sure, Sister Mary, you are as skilled with them as I, so you may do up the arm and I will assist you." He praised her work when they were finished ("as pretty a job as I have ever seen") and helped her clear away the scraps of cloth.

121

Then he took a large square of cloth, folded it into a triangle, enfolded my arm in it, and tied the ends around my neck. "This will ease the arm by supporting it, and will help prevent it bumping into things, while at the same time freeing the other arm for its tasks," he explained. "You should take it off only when in bed or sitting in a place which can support the arm. For so I learned from the mighty Guy de Chauliac."[xlix]

"You are old," he said bluntly to me, "but if you follow my advice your arm will heal straight and strong as it was before it was broken. You are to start no penitential diet while the bone is healing. In six or eight weeks, have the arm looked at to see if it is still in place and healing as it ought. In ten weeks, perhaps, the splint can be removed. Do you understand? Not before."

"Yes, that is quite clear." I fancied there was already some easing of the pain I had suffered. Such a little fuss to start a cure! I said to him, "Since you set the bone, I should like you to look at it. Will you be near Deerfield in six or eight weeks?"

Before my eyes he turned back into a beggar. He hung his head and mumbled, "I go where the pickings are good, m'lady, and I do not know where that might be in six weeks' time." He waited patiently for me to send him away.

I made a sudden decision. "But — there is no need for you to go anyplace! Deer Abbey, like many others, has often taken one or two veterans of the army under its wing. We grant them a small pension and find a place for them to stay. They have two gowns and a pair of shoes a year of the Abbey. It would please me, Lucas Barber, if you would allow Deer Abbey to grant you its pension. You, unlike the others, could earn your keep as chirurgeon to the Abbey. Is that an acceptable proposition?"

The humble beggar was gone again, tossed aside like outworn gloves. (And we never saw him again either, for he was a proud fellow, our Lucas Barber!) He bowed awkwardly, and said "I am most profoundly grateful to you, my lady! But I can better your offer: I will need only half a pair of shoes a year — *and* I am as good with injured animals as with people!"

"Splendid! Agreed!" I cried. "Go now; Elizabeth will find you space in our guest-house until other arrangements can be made." There is a broken spirit there I would you could mend, I thought.

"Thank you, my lady." He bowed again and left with Elizabeth, Sister Mary in his wake, still glowing gently from his praise. "You were too kind to him, my lady!" scolded Sister Harley when they were gone.

"I know," I sighed, leaning back in my chair, but I smiled.

"What if he's married?" she persisted.

"Oh, he probably is, with sixteen children besides! I don't care a brass button, let him bring his wife *and* his children!"

"He'll have no respect for you," she warned.

"No, but he'll love me for giving him back his dignity, and will pray hard for my soul when I die. And after what I have done this day," I cried in anguish, "that appears a great bargain whatever the cost! Thanks be to God for him, I say; and *you* may be silent!"

"Yes, my lady," said Sister Harley, affronted. "With your kind permission, my lady!" And she took herself out of the room.

I rested until None, when Mellie came to help me dress. She declared herself very satisfied with my arm, its pain having diminished remarkably. I prayed carefully the prayers of None; and ate lightly of a fine dinner: Leeks creamed in almond milk; pike from our own fishpond in rosemary sauce; herb custard, made with eggs and milk and greens with sweet, savory and pungent herbs; wafers and hipocras for dessert.

I slept again a little bit before Vespers, watched over Father Hugh with Sister Emma until Compline, and slept soundly until Matins and Lauds.

We began at Matins and Lauds the formal Office of the Dead, gathering in our calefactory around the open coffin. "Why is it that Thou wilt make so noble a thing of man, wilt pay so much heed to him?" we asked at Matins, and prayed at Lauds, "We humbly entreat Thee for the soul of Thy servant Hugh, who at Thy bidding departed from this world."

At Chapter Saturday morning my ladies all expressed themselves content with my decision to take on Lucas Barber, even Sister Harley (who had discovered he was a bachelor). He had appeared at all our prayers, grave and reserved, and did not speak unless first spoken to. Yet he did not have the shocked and humbled air of the just-rescued. Like a cat, he had landed on his feet – I mean foot -- and I admired him for it.

Sister Harley was assigned to supervise Austin in arranging for repairs to the wool barn. Two looms had been dragged out during the fire, but one was badly charred and probably not usable. Nothing else was saved; we lost about fifty pounds of wool (about half of it spun into yarn), three looms, a dozen distaffs, four dye vats and various odds and ends stored in the barn. Will Calendrer burned his hands saving the two looms, but not seriously.

The bell could be repaired; the crack was not serious.

My ladies agreed that Papion was too young for his job of Porter. These unsettled times called for an older head. Sister Harley suggested Tiffany Tybalt be given the post temporarily while a search went out for a permanent Porter.

"What about Papion? What shall we do with him?" asked Sister Clara in her musical voice.

"Set him to work in the kitchen," suggested Sister Mildred dryly

"Give him a penny and turn him out the gate he guarded so poorly," offered Sister Alys, with an almost rude indifference.

"Buy him an apprenticeship," I proposed — to a horrified silence. Finally Sister Harley spoke. "You suggest we *reward* him for incompetence?"

"No, I suggest we find something he *can* do. As I recall, we were all very fond of Papion before Thursday night. He is a freeman, literate and bright. But he is also an orphan without money to buy an apprenticeship. It is true that he is somewhat flighty, but he is honest and devout." They gaped at me, remembering my fury of the previous morning at the man I was now praising. "He also has a good ear for a tune," I concluded, somewhat lamely.

They were reluctantly convinced to look into it. When we told Papion of our plans, he fell hard onto his knees in astonished thanks.

"Another grateful one," I thought. He ended up going to a bell-maker in Oxford.

After Sext I took a walk around our orchard behind the cloister. The late summer sun was warm and there was a sleepy sound of humming bees. I could not stay long — there was the church to clean today, and Austin to convince we could not afford to make the wool barn's new roof of slate, and something had to be done about Angharad — but I laid all concerns aside for these few minutes to refresh myself in the scent of late roses and ripening apples.

When I finally turned back towards the cloister gate, I saw the great white swan old Jack reported, resting prettily near the wall of the warming room. But when I approached it rose and spread its large wings and threatened me with gesture and hiss until I withdrew. There was no sign of a mate and it was the wrong time of year for a nest of young, so I thought its behavior peculiar. I wondered how long it would stay. I was afraid of it, uneasily recalling stories of men killed by swans.

I went from the orchard to the church where my ladies were already sweeping, scrubbing and dusting. Sister Emma had found the missing marble nose behind the north choir stalls and had wrapped it in a soft dustcloth. I gave it to our Sacrist, Sister Alison, to keep until she could arrange to have it cemented in place. Then I took a dustcloth and began to remove cobwebs from the carved wainscoting of the Sacristy.

I heard feet shuffling behind me and turned, startled (it sounded like Father Hugh) to see Father Clement hurrying towards us. "The Bishop!" he gasped. "Coming up the lane! Be here soon!"

My ladies quickly gathered round. As usual, Sister Harley was the most impeccably dressed, so I sent her at once to the guest-house so someone could greet the bishop if he arrived before the rest of us. We put away our brooms and cloths and hurried to sluice our hands and faces and change to garb appropriate to a bishop's visit.

Because of my arthritic slowness and bandaged arm, I was last to arrive at the great hall of our guest-house. My ladies had completed formal greetings and were gathered around the great carved chair in which the bishop sat, listening breathlessly to tales out of court. There was with him a tall, red-headed priest I did not at once recognize.

I bent my left knee before Bishop Morys and kissed his ring and said I hoped he'd been made welcome. He'd grown somewhat fatter since last I saw him, but was otherwise swarthy as ever, with the same unlovely moist red mouth.

His protuberant brown eyes noted my splinted arm. "Your Abbey has suffered much, and you yourself were not spared," he said in an affected lisp.[1] "I *do* hope your noble young friend the Duke of Gloucester will be able to protect you from further suffering, my dear Lady Margaret." He shot an unfriendly glance at the ring still attached to my left thumb — no doubt my eager ladies had told its story to him. I recalled Bishop Morys had a Woodville connection somewhere, and the Queen's party was not friendly to the stiff remnant of feudalism whose gift I bore. From what I knew of each, I would take the Duke over the Queen any day![li]

"I thank your lordship for your concern. But the man who caused us to suffer is dead, and his men are, with one or two exceptions, awaiting the arrival of the King's justices." He gently helped me to my feet, and I continued, "And all is not for nothing. I have learned a good lesson from this sorrow."

"Oh?" He politely assumed a look of interest.

"For all I have seen and heard of dangers and treasons and unjust suffering throughout our Kingdom, I thought Deer Abbey the one safe place, a place almost like heaven. I forgot its peace must be guarded, just as it must anyplace else on earth. There is no heaven on earth; so long as we live, a misstep, a moment of carelessness, even a rumor may destroy us."

I was speaking to and of myself, but Bishop Morys looked disturbed, and shifted uneasily in his seat. "Ha-rum, a wise sermon, prettily put!" he said. "But, my lady, did you notice who I brought with me? Look at this strapping fellow closely: Do you know him?"

I looked at the tall redhead with the priest's tonsure, broad peasant face and merry blue eyes. "Why, it's James Herriot!" I cried. Now Father James, of course, but the same happy villein who had wiped his face on my wimple sixteen years ago! He bent to give me a solemn kiss of peace, but the eye farthest from the bishop winked as he stepped away from me. How well he looked! But the flaming hair around his tonsure still curled incorrigibly as ever.

"Are you here to see your brother and sister?" I asked him.

"No, I'm here to say Father Hugh's funeral, if that's all right with Father Clement," he replied. "Father Hugh was very, very good to me."

"Of course, my son," said Father Clement, pleased. He hated funerals.

The bishop spoke up. "We had set out from Banbury for Swindon when your messenger overtook us and led us on a trail I didn't know existed, which cut several hours off the journey here.

Remarkable fellow, Bodrey. But I still have to get to Swindon as soon as possible, so I will reconcile your church first thing in the morning and be on my way. Father James can stay behind to do the funeral, and catch up with me in Swindon." He turned to the young priest. "Have I got it right?"

"Yes, my lord."

"I don't know what I'd do without Jamie as secretary. He keeps me on a busy schedule, but so long as I listen to him I get everywhere on time. Don't know why I'm not thin as a rake, the traveling I do," complained his lordship jovially.

But he showed us why over supper, where he exhibited great skill as a trencherman. (We had roast capons with a black sauce made of their livers.)

Over a sweet wine Bishop Morys turned to business and directed Father James to help Sister Alison produce the needed articles for the ceremony of reconciliation in the morning: "Put in your northern cloister walk, near the main door into the church, a faldstool with white coverings. I brought my folding chair with me, but we'll need a second inside the church. You have one? Good. We'll need a white cloth large enough for the faldstool to stand on, a small table with a large vessel of clean water, an empty vessel for holy water, a small quantity of salt on a dish, a sprinkler made of hyssop, a ladle, a towel, my copy of the *Roman Pontifical*, and a small candle stick with a candle.

"Before the altar in the church will be the second faldstool also with white coverings and also on a white cloth, with a cushion for me to kneel on before it, a crucifix, candlesticks and altar cloths for the altar near at hand, music for the singers on the gospel side and on the epistle side another table with the same items as out in the cloister walk and in addition a cruet of wine and a dish of finely sifted ashes.[lii]

"I want Father James as Master of Ceremonies, Father Clement and whoever is rector of St. Michael's in Deerfield" ("Father Christopher," I interposed gently) "as subdeacon. I have already sent one of my men to speak to him, Lady Margaret; do not worry about sending for him. I leave to the competent Sister Alison to find me a cross-bearer, two acolytes, a holy water bearer, four altar boys who can be trusted to fetch and carry my mitre, crozier, book and candle, and perhaps a few extras just in case. And, of course, some or all of you ladies to chant the psalms and responses."

Doubtless Bishop Morys had recently consulted his *Pontifical* about the ceremony of reconciliation, but his perfect and effortless recollection was very impressive. I suddenly remembered the bishop had had no helpful uncle able to give him a boost up the ecclesiastical ladder; here was an artless display of the grasp of detail he was capable of which had proved its own boost. Behind the uncomely face was also a kind heart; there was no need for him to allow Father James to stay behind for the funeral.

The next morning, Sunday, immediately after Prime, my ladies and I gathered to watch an invasion of our cloister by men in larger numbers than it had suffered since it was re-built 160 years ago. Lady Angharad had sent her chaplain to act as subdeacon, so Father Christopher was named cross-bearer. Lady Angharad would be there in time for the funeral, said her chaplain.

When everyone was in position in the north walk of the cloister by the church, the bishop appeared, wearing his surplice-like rochet and the hooded cape that marked his status as our Ordinary. But he was immediately borne off by a procession to be properly vested in the Sacristy — which in our church was located in the rear.

When he returned he was all in white and gold, with a floor-length white cope embroidered in gold, a gold mitre, and carrying a crozier flashing with gold and gems. He sat on his faldstool before the door to the church porch and there was a lengthy pause.

"Has he fallen asleep?" whispered tiny Sister Emma anxiously. "No, he is gathering his strength," I whispered back. "The ceremony is complicated, but must be done exactly right or the demons presently occupying our church will not flee."

Bishop Morys stood at a signal from Father James and went to bless the water on the small table in a rather elaborate ceremony. I noticed Tiff's grandson Nab had been selected to ladle the water into its special ewer. He was a pretty child when thoroughly scrubbed, and his hand was steady.

Bishop Morys intoned "*Asperges me*" to start the chanters (Sisters Alys, Harley, Clara and Alison) who took up the chant, "Sprinkle me with hyssop, o Lord, and I shall be clean; wash me and I shall be whiter than snow," and continued with the 50th Psalm, "Have mercy on me, O Lord, according to Thy great mercies ..."

The bishop, preceded by a cross-bearer, the acolytes, the deacon and subdeacon, led the chanters counterclockwise around the church and cemetery, and he dipped the branch of hyssop into the holy water (into which a little blessed salt had been added) and sprinkled the walls of the church and headstones of the cemetery. We spectators trailed after. I was surprised to note the swan made no threatening gestures, but watched us pass with an almost friendly interest.

In the cemetery the bishop prayed in brisk lisping Latin that God "our Potter" who was the "price of this field,"[liii] might reconcile this cemetery, the "resting place of Thy pilgrims," and at the end of time resurrect "the bodies both of those already buried and those who will henceforth be buried at this place."

There was a small gate beside our charnel house, seldom used because it led but to a narrow place between the cemetery wall and the outermost wall of the Abbey. Now it was standing open in readiness for Bishop Morys and us, who walked along it until we came to the north wall of the church, where he resumed sprinkling until he came round to where we began.

Then we all went inside the church to continue the ceremony. The bishop exorcised and blessed in turn the salt, the ashes and the water at the little table, then mixed salt and ashes and put the mixture in the water. The wine was blessed and added to the mixture. Nab of the steady hand filled the ewer with the mix and handed it with a bow to the bishop, who walked around the church sprinkling it high on the walls with a fresh branch of hyssop while the chanters floated Psalm 67 on the plaintive notes of plainsong: "May the Lord be gracious to us and bless us . ." with the antiphon, "May God rise up and His enemies be scattered, and let them that hate Him flee from his sight!"

The second time around the church, Bishop Morys sprinkled the lower walls and the third time the floor — giving special attention to that place near the foot of the altar where we found Lady Bertille.

Psalms 42 and 67 (again) were chanted, and then the bishop, quickening as he neared the end, rapidly prayed an oddly-formed prayer, full of little parentheses or asides, to God whose church, the mother of all nations, gathered from the ends of the earth, decorated by the merits of his holy martyrs, being already embellished by a variety of peoples, [God] please bless this altar, adorned with relics of his saints, them helping God to bless the altar, and also sanctify the church and the prayers His faithful people offer Him in it. This he prayed to Him who reigns with God the Father and the Holy Spirit, God forever and ever. There was a solemn and most heartfelt "Amen" breathed so gustily the two infulae hanging down behind the bishop's mitre stirred in the breeze — or so it was said later, over mugs of ale in Deerfield

The bishop then returned to the sacristy to vest himself for Mass. Most of the rest of us, since we were to attend Father Hugh's funeral Mass shortly, left the church.

As I entered the west cloister walk, I overheard the childish voice of Sister Emma. She, Sister Mary, Sister Alys and our young novice Lady Cicely were laughing heartily about something as they moved down the walk ahead of me, so I drifted up from behind to discover what was amusing them. "Fourteen times! I counted fourteen times!" said Sister Emma in a thin, suppressed shriek. "Put the mitre on, go here, say a prayer, take the mitre off, bow, put the mitre on, take the mitre off to exorcise the salt, put it on to bless the salt, take it off to exorcise the water, put it on —"

"To bless the water. Am I correct?" I finished for her.

The four jumped guiltily and turned to face me. My anger had risen from its ashes and must have blazed in my face from the way they paled. "You laugh at things you do not understand!" I said. I kept my voice low and the effort made it tremble. "When you have studied the history of God's church, when you *understand* Latin, not just gabble it from rote, *then* you may laugh at the oddities of a ceremony you have never seen before and — *pray God* — may never see again!"

They dropped to their knees and began to murmur apologies. "You will come to me at Chapter tomorrow morning in just such a pose!" I said coldly and walked away.

In a very short while I was called to say goodbye to the bishop — Titivillus must have escaped another beating thanks to Bishop Morys[liv] — and watched him mount his tall and magnificently caparisoned white mule. They headed out the main gate, the bishop, a well-armed bodyguard of six men, and a trail of Sumter horses, servants and dogs.

Back in the inner courtyard I saw Austin standing on the steps of the guest-house, regaling a cluster of my ladies, servants and villeins with stories of Father Hugh. They were all in their best dress and their faces were joyous.

"He was wearing that shoddy old armor Thurston Smith made for him twenty years ago. Remember when he was made almoner of the Abbey and discovered almoners not only fed beggars, they were in charge of security? It cost him two years of Masses for Thurston's mother's soul to get that armor and it's like nothing any man of arms ever wore before." There was laughter at this as I drew nearer.

"Anyway, there he was in that armor, walking up and down on the roof of the gatehouse, throwing suspicious glances up and down the lane every so often while Pap and I sneered at him. But he kept telling us hair-raising stories of ambushes and sneak attacks he'd got from old soldiers, and got us both stirred up until we almost hoped Sir Ranulf *would* ride up looking for trouble!

"Pap and I joined him walking up and down, looking out for any sign of mischief. I asked him how Lady Bertille was, and he said she was sore hurt, but was a brave lady who would not say who hurt her because she didn't want him attacking *us* like he attacked *her*."

There was sympathetic murmuring over this.

"Then he got very serious and said that if we had done something about Sir Ranulf when he first started terrorizing our villeins, as we should have, we would have saved ourselves a lot of trouble — including this mess with poor Lady Bertille. 'Villeins may be the property of those gently born, he said, but they have souls like the rest of us — and they are our responsibility. I am ashamed of us,' he said."

The words were like a buffet to my heart. I knew Austin just quoted Father Hugh; I had heard those turns of phrase many a Sunday. But rage swelled in my breast.

"Austin, how dare you repeat such words of criticism to my face?" I shouted. "And why do the rest of you stand there blubbering over them? Stop it at once!" I felt dizzy with anger.

Sister Harley came immediately to me and took me gently in her arms. "Oh, my lady," she soothed me, "we are weeping because we all are to blame, and because Austin is telling of the last hours of Father Hugh, whom we dearly loved!"

"But I loved him, too!" I said in some confusion. "And I don't want him to go away from us!"

There was a little silence at this, and Sister Alison asked in a mildly puzzled voice, "But he's already gone, isn't he?"

I started to laugh at my stupid remark. "Yes, of course he is, my dear." Suddenly the terrible weight in my chest evaporated. "He's gone, he's *gone!*" I wailed, and I could at last weep for the losses I had endured.

We gathered in the little court by the priest's house; we would go into the church through the rearmost door, through the Sacristy/bell tower, because I did not want men and layfolk unnecessarily traipsing through our cloister.

Sister Emma, startled, pointed at the top of the bell tower: our swan had moved his resting place from the outside wall of the calefactory to one of the outer corners of the tower. "It's a sign, I'm sure," she said, but of what no one could say, of course.

Father James Herriot threw open the door of the church like one about to greet an old friend. He walked around the plain wooden coffin — how little it was! — and sprinkled holy water on it: "Eternal rest grant unto him, O Lord," he prayed.

"And let perpetual light shine upon him," we replied strongly.

Then the coffin was carried into the church on the shoulders of Tiff, Bodrey, Papion and Jack, John Freemantle's son. Their slightly exalted expressions were caused at least in part by having won the several battles fought for the honor. "... go out to meet him, every angel of the Lord," asked Father James. How glad, I thought, heaven must be to have him home at last!

Because he was a priest, the Mass of All Souls was celebrated instead of the Mass of the Dead. There was a reading from a letter of St. Paul to the Corinthians: "Where then, death, is thy victory; where ... thy sting? It is sin that gives death its sting, just as it is the law that gives sin its power ..." I glanced over at Lady Angharad, sitting stiff and expressionless on a stool brought for her. It was living that stung Angharad.

"... Thou gavest him the gift of faith; do not withhold the reward of his belief," intoned Father James in beautiful Latin. His pleasant round face was meant to laugh or rage; to see it pale and controlled was more terrible than to see it abandoned to grief.

"... accept and bless these gifts, these holy things we owe to you, these sacred unblemished things," went the prayers of the Offertory. Would that include a small priest's soul? I never saw or heard of him doing a wicked thing. He broke a shocking number of butter and jam pots, and never ate a meal without leaving traces of all its courses about his person, but he was unfailingly kind to everyone — except unrepentant sinners, whom he often disconcerted with that unexpected piercing look of his.

"I will wash my hands among the innocent ... do not number my soul among ... those men of blood, whose guilty hands are full of bribes ... I will go my way blamelessly ..." He had used his quarterstaff on occasion with a fierce pleasure; and in that was a man of blood, a warrior. But he told me once that the business with the worm and hook almost spoiled fishing for him, and I laughed at him and said he ought to be a Franciscan.

I had been absently twisting the Duke's ring around my thumb just then, when I suddenly realized it had come loose, and I looked down to see it shining in the palm of my right hand, half hidden by the splint that bound my wrist. I wrapped it in my damp handkerchief and pushed it up my sleeve.

"In Him there was life, and that life was the light of men. And the light shines in the darkness, and the darkness cannot overpower it." Then there was the little black hole in the floor for his coffin. I remember the grumbling struggle to reset the paving stones of the floor after he was lowered into it. I remember not crying.

We came out of the church the same way we went in. "Look!" someone shouted, pointing upward. The swan was making a big circle around the bell tower. It flew off to the east (and did not return, thank God), and I turned to speak to Sister Harley about the harvest that must begin at dawn tomorrow.[lv]

Thy Will Be Done

by Margaret of Shaftesbury

1485: The World in Brief

Japan is being torn by a civil war which will last 100 years.

Mohammed II, founder of the great Ottoman Empire, died four years ago.

Under the rule of clever Lorenzo the Magnificent, Florence has become one of the most beautiful and prosperous cities in Italy. (The Medici family's huge fortune was built on banking and moneylending. The three balls of a pawnbroker come from the Medici coat of arms.)

Innocent VIII is Pope. Last year he issued very severe measures against witches and magicians in Germany. The Waldensian heretics are becoming strong enough to attract his attention.

Ferdinand and Isabella jointly rule all of Spain except Navarre in the north and Moorish Granada in the south. The Spanish Inquisition began in 1478, its stated aim to discover converted Jews who still practice their old religion in private.

Ships have been setting out from Europe, to explore the oceans in the name of trade. The Age of Exploration is underway. The Portuguese have explored the Congo River, and have settlements on the Gold Coast (Ghana).

Hungary, having captured Vienna and lower Austria this year, has become the most powerful state in central Europe.

Charles the Bold of Burgundy, who had ambitions to expand his duchy into a kingdom by conquering the lands which lay between its two parts, was defeated and killed at Nancy, Lorraine, in

January of 1477. Burgundy still prefers England to its nominal overlord, France.

William Caxton has been operating his printing press at Westminster for nine years. Last year he published Malory's *Morte d'Arthur*.

Richard III has been King of England since July of 1483. Near Market Bosworth in Leicestershire with his army, he succeeded at last this morning in bringing the rebel Henry Tudor to battle. It is August 22, 1485.

Thy Will Be Done

With much nervous anxiety Sisters Alys, Valeria, Julia, and Ursula have helped me cross to Shearing Meadow to watch Papion cast our new bell. The old bell, whose repair has failed repeatedly over the fifteen years since it first cracked, lies in pieces here, waiting to be melted and incorporated with additional bronze. Assisting in transporting me were Austin, Gib and Pip, with heartfelt advice and moral support from Sisters Agnes, Mary, Susanna, and Lucy, not to mention Father Edward, a stray shepherd, our groom, our old laundress, two stableboys, a gardener, the gatekeeper and three villeins who had come to sell us a cow. One would think they were moving the abbey church.

Of course I will admit that I am almost fabulously old, being able to recall quite clearly the capture of the Scottish King James I and the Council of Pisa in the time of Henry IV, and that of late I have become frail. But though my vision is clouded, my mind is clear — when they do not fuddle me with unnecessary detail — and my hearing good, provided they do not mumble. Perhaps they fuss because this is the first time I have gone outside the walls of Deer Abbey in seven years or more. But it is only the briefest of journeys to go out the gate and across the road, and their fussing irritates me and makes me cross. A mere journey across the road shouldn't be treated as a pilgrimage — all I need is an arm to lean on, a person to bring my chair, and another to carry a coverlet and cushion. But they come in dozens, and fuss, and nag one another, and

I begin to feel like a caterpillar being carried off by ants.

With such an army, each demanding a share in the task, it is small wonder it takes near half an hour to conclude matters. My chair is so laden with cushions and blankets as to be uncomfortable. They seat me and thrust cushions under my feet and behind my back and under each elbow and cover me to the eyes with draperies and quarrel over the placement of each until I am utterly out of temper.

"Enough!" I say at last. "Go, all of you, go back to the abbey. If you think fussing with me will excuse one of you from your assigned tasks, you had best think again! Leave be, Mary! Pip, if you touch that blanket again, I shall demote you to swineherd!"

There is a murmur of apologies, and I sigh and gesture forgiveness. "Ursula and Austin may stay. The rest of you, go away!" Off they go, saying, "Well, if you hadn't —" and "We were only trying —" and "You shouldn't've insisted —" in fierce undertones at one another.

Austin takes up a position on my right, and Ursula moves a spare cushion to a place near my feet and sits down with a sigh. She is just sixteen, newly professed, and trying hard not to not to be proud of her current assignment as my chaplain.[lvi]

She came to us as a child, good and gentle, but with a twisted back. Her father could not find a husband for her, and so sent her to us. She seems content. I, too, came to Deer Abbey as a youngling. I remember ...

It had been raining for two days, and now it was nearly dark. I was sitting on the pommel of a man's saddle, he big and warm against my back, but the rain cold on my front. The abbey wall appeared, a pale flatness in the dimness; then the greater shape of the gatehouse loomed up. The man spoke to the porter but I was too dazed with tiredness to understand the words. Then I was lifted down and carried into a room and put before a fireplace with a meager fire. The man was sent away and a lady all in black came in. She held a candle close to my face and said, "What is your name, child?"

" Mar'get."

"You must say, 'my lady,' child."

"Mar'get, my lady. Is my mama here?"

"No, you have left your mama forever." I remember crying. I was four years old.

I had been brought to Deer Abbey at the command of a father I had never seen, who sent as dower (to insure their acceptance of me) a deed to the Manor of Broughton. Edmund, first Duke of York, son of Edward III, was my father — and my mother was a serving maid, one of the many all too susceptible to the notorious Plantagenet charm. I was the daughter of a prince, a boast greatly tempered by the fact that I was also a bantling.

I don't remember Ursula crying, but then, she was ten and possibly disappointed with the secular world. The cloister has its disappointments, too, of course. And its surprises.

Sitting in the Chapter House, nervous and waiting. Sun streaming through the windows, a thin, unwarming winter sun. Lady Eleanor had died, and we must pray and vote for a new abbess. The two major candidates were Sister Eustachia and Sister Elizabeth, and they each had campaigned vigorously, albeit discreetly, for the position. Sister Eustachia was tall and slim, with long white hands and proud bearing, the daughter of an Earl and a niece of Sir John de Cynegil, whose family ties with Deer Abbey go back centuries. Sister Elizabeth was plump and sweet, efficient and kind, a far more capable administrator than the forbidding Sister Eustachia, but without noble connections. Who would win?

There were rumors that the servants were hoping for Elizabeth but betting on Eustachia, which had amused some of us when we heard about it. "Not less than four ballots," predicted Sister Joan boldly, "and possibly six, before we decide who it shall be." That being the case, none of us wished to declare ourselves too early, and so on the first ballot we each secretly decided to vote for someone else entirely, someone without a chance to win. Unfortunately, they all decided I was that one: Thus does God laugh at our jokes.

There was much poorly-concealed dismay at the result — and the normally purely-formal exclamations of reluctance and denial of worthiness expected of a new abbess had in my case a clear ring of sincerity. King Henry VI confirmed my election, but we had to get a dispensation, *super defecta natalium*, from the bishop before I could be installed as abbess.[lvii] When the crozier was put into my trembling hands, I burst into tears, so frightened was I.

There is a sound like dragons breathing in the meadow; I start. Bellows. Austin had explained that Papion would set up furnaces in the meadow in which the copper and tin would be melted along with the old bell. But it still sounds like dragons. St. Margaret came out of a dragon whole.[lviii] "Where is my crozier?"

"Here, my lady," says Austin, our steward, finding it leaning on the back of my chair and handing it to me. He is a good man, but I miss John Freemantle, our former steward, dead these ten years now. His grandson John is currently with King Richard as a groom.

I have carried this crozier fifty-one years and six months; they will close my dead fingers around it before they put me under the floor of our church — but not yet, not yet. I have some things to do, first.

"Papion, where are you?"

"Here, Lady Margaret," he replies.

"Come here and tell me what you are doing." I have followed this mysterious business of making a bell with great interest.

"Yes, madame," he says, coming to kneel before me. I remember when he knelt to declare himself in my mercy fifteen years ago this very month, having so neglected his duties that men of murderous purpose easily got past him. How indignant my ladies were when I decided his punishment was to be apprenticed to a belleter. But here he is, still with the tow-colored hair and brilliant blue eyes of his youth, but having added the powerful shoulders and countless burn scars of his profession. He is a fine craftsman whose bells call people to worship, warn of danger, stave off lightning, aid the soul in passing and tell listeners a Christian has died. Surely that is recompense more valuable than a year of flagellation in sackcloth and ashes.

"... ask me something?" says Papion, recalling me from my musings. Not that he hasn't had to do with ashes; one can barely see the blue of his tunic for the smoke and ash leavings about him.

"Yes, tell me, where is the great mold you made for the bell?" "Here, at your feet, madame," he replies. There is a circular area of stones at my feet.

"Here?"

"Madame, we dug a pit for the mold, and put the bell mold into it — "

"I know that," I interrupt proudly. Austin described the process to me, how Papion dug the pit and made a foundation, set four posts to mark it and filled it in again. Then the mold was carried across and put on top of the earth between the posts. Very carefully, bit by bit, the earth was removed, first on one side then the other, while, guided by the posts, the mold sank down to come safely to rest on the foundation. Thus it was saved from being lowered by ropes, with consequent danger of dropping and breakage.[lix]

"You filled the pit with stones?" I ask.

"Nay, madame; it is inside an oven; we are baking the mold and when it is red hot, we will pour in the metal, which we are now melting. We buried it with enough wood to burn for a night and a day. Do you hear the bellows? There are two furnaces in which we will reduce the metal to a liquid, and two of your villeins are hard at work at them."

"Of course I hear them! Do you think me deaf? How long will this take?"

"We are some hours away, yet."

"Thank you, Papion." He rises and returns to his labors.

"Do I hear riders?" I ask a minute later, trying to look around Ursula.

"Yes, my lady," says Austin. "It's Sir Christopher and three riders. He's been to Banbury."

One does not travel alone in England nowadays, even when one is as brave and strong as Sir Christopher. I remember when he first came to the Cotswolds, at the King's bidding, to take over Angharad's property when her father was killed fighting with Edward IV, leaving no male heir.[lx] Christopher was a younger son, and had been meant for a priest, so was over-learned and somewhat shy for his size. Besides not being having the training of a knight at that time, he likewise had few of the accomplishments of a courtier. But ill-equipped as he was in such matters, he took one look at Angharad and decided he was in love. I could not see why, as she was like a dry stick during that first encounter, utterly lacking in conversation or other show of intelligence.

Angharad had twice offered to take vows as a nun. I had refused to allow it. We had no need of such poor company as she would provide, nor is the cloister a place of refuge from secular pressures — we have most of them and more of our own. Besides, I had memories of the flame that once burned within her, and hoped to rekindle it in time. So I encouraged Lord Christopher to call again.

Soon I was sorry. Trying to impress her, he acquired a stallion he could barely handle, and which was a menace in our stables. He bought a lute he could not tune and took lessons from a charlatan. He began to wear the most outrageous fashions, jupons so short and hose so tight that, had he been Jewish, the world could have been told it by merely watching his approach. And he composed terrible songs in her honor, which he insisted on singing to us all, praising her sunken eyes, lifeless hair and colorless lips in terms so mendacious I was concerned for his soul.

Angharad came to me one day with a bundle of flowers she could not have kept in a hogshead and a sheaf of poems — he had expanded into poetry — and tossed the whole onto my table. "What am I to *do* with him?" she demanded.

"Do not yield until you are sure he is sincere," I said with great earnestness, and, after a startled blink, she saw the joke and began to laugh. I joined in, my laughter colored by joy at this sign of the old Angharad.

He neglected his duties at her manors during this time of ardent courtship, and then vanished for a week, trying to catch up. When he reappeared, it was as if a different soul inhabited his body. His brief jupon was changed for a modest houppeland, he was worn and dusty, and there were no flowers or bad poems to offer.

It took Angharad only a few minutes to discover what the matter was. With the harvest about to begin, he found that his steward had sold (with his unwitting approval) several workhorses and a piece of land on which his granary barn stood. Some of the money had gone for a horse and new apparel, the rest into the steward's pocket.

Moreover, smelling weakness, the villeins had organized themselves to resist the boon reap days necessary to complete the harvest. When he had tried to reason with them, they became unruly.

This was Angharad's land he was bringing to ruin, and she was not about to allow that. "Fire the steward at once," she counseled. "Ask John Freemantle to recommend another. And don't argue with the villeins; there's no time for that. The harvest must begin on time, or we will lose most of it. Arrest the ringleaders and hold them against the good behavior of the others until the harvest is in. Only then can we deal with their demands. Meanwhile, offer to rent the horses they are not required to bring as part of their harvest duties. And the abbey has horses we may borrow. See if whoever bought the barn will rent all or part of it to us. Failing that, hold a barn-raising bene.[lxi] They've owed us one for years."

This was a new Angharad, one with color in her cheeks and a wit or two in her head. She came with him as he set about dealing with his crises. She had a keen eye for detail, and saw to them, down to getting a pair of cats to keep the new barn free of mice. He quickly came to realize that a frail, ethereal angel was all very well for dreams and moonstruck goofs, but when one was trying to run a couple of manors with hardly any background or training in such things, a bright and capable woman was much more the thing.

They have three sturdy children. The oldest, James, has gone now to Sir Alwyn's castle to be taught the ways of a knight. He is a careful, level-headed child, subtle-minded even at the age of twelve. The manors will remain in his family through even these slippery times, I am sure.

The riders stop along the road, and one dismounts and comes to me. "My lady," he says now, bending the knee to me, a glittery silver shape in the sunlight. It is Sir Christopher, in armor.

"Have you news of the King?" I ask.

"Nothing much, m'lady. He is near Leicester, where it is hoped he will tackle Henry Tudor soon."

"Yes, Freemantle is with him; he promised to send word when the traitor is conquered."

"May that be soon, m'lady; England is sore distressed."

"Amen, amen to that. How is Angharad?"

"Very well. She wants to come and see you, but her time is very near, and she mustn't travel."

"Remind her of her promise that if it is a girl, she will name her Margaret and give her to Deer Abbey as a nun."

He smiles. "I will, but Maud is already showing true piety. Perhaps you'll have her instead."

But I have my heart set on a Margaret, so I say, "Well, piety in one only six years old is charming, but let's wait a bit to see if it lasts. How is little John?"

"He continues very boisterous. And as brave a child as I have ever seen, m'lady. He rode his pony through Wychwood to Dowse last week with a merry whistle and not one fearful look — and he won't be five until November."

I smile and nod; I like John very much, but I am glad it is James who will inherit. These are not the times for brave and merry men. "Will you stay and watch us cast our new bell?"

Sir Christopher rises. "I would be delighted to do so; but I must get home, to give Angharad her orange. This is the third one for this pregnancy. I had to ride clean to Banbury for it; do you think I indulge her too much?"

"Nay, not her."

He bends to kiss my withered cheek. "You're right," he murmurs, "not her." Sir Christopher has broken the rules of courtly love: he loves his wife with that passion one supposedly cannot have for one he is bound by God to honor.

I tasted an orange once. Sister Harley was sent one, and she shared it with me. It reminded me of a rose hip beverage I used to brew as a treatment for colds.[lxii] I miss Sister Harley.

In a few minutes the clatter of horses fades and all I can hear is the rush of the bellows and Papion's urging on of his helpers. A souvenir of times past rests in my hand. It is a gold ring, given to me by an unexpected visitor, Richard Duke of Gloucester, now King Richard III. It was meant to be sold, in payment of accommodation and supplies offered to him on that occasion. But I kept it, and I was still wearing it when Sir Ranulf Fitzralph was about to kill me, and the sight of that ring, given by one who could not be bought or frightened, saved my life. (Not that sparing me saved him!)

I've been tempted several times to sell the ring, but I haven't, not when our kitchen lost its roof in a fire, nor when murrain wiped out half our sheep, nor even when Richard wrote asking for money to finance his campaigns against Warwick. (I sold my mare and my unicorn tapestry instead, that time.)

He wore cloth shoes with white roses embroidered on them, shining in the light of many candles. Candles glowing, great candles, whose heat I feel on my face –

I start; Papion has come to check the fire burning under the bell. Heat rises to brush my face when he opens the top of the furnace, for I am seated close to the edge of the pit. I must not fall; God save me from the pit. How terrible to burn forever. Fire hot enough to melt metal ...

I remember a blacksmith in Deerfield Village. Broad and black he was, with huge arms and a filthy leather apron. He could take raw cold iron and make steel of it. He made horseshoes with fire and a hammer, sparks flying, the metal white hot, cooling to red. He plunged them, hissing, into water. He made knives and plowshares and wheel rims. Even the grownups were in awe of him. He made me a horseshoe ring I wore for three days until the Novice Mistress caught me with it and beat me soundly for superstition[lxiii] and pride.

I look at the ring, hidden in my palm. Pride, deadliest of sins, has again been my downfall. Slowly, over the past year, I have been divesting myself of all my personal possessions, my beloved tapestries, my set of fine steel needles, my ivory rosary. As a Benedictine, I ought not to have any to start with, but that part of the Rule has never been much honored among nuns. I have visited abbeys in which obedientiaries have their own room, with each her own servants and chests full of personal possessions to which each has her own key and the abbess has none. I would not allow us to fall that far, but fall we have, and being better than the worst is not good enough. I feel my day of judgment coming. All I now own is my habit and my crosier — and this ring. Richard gave it to me for the abbey, but I put it on my thumb and no one ever questioned my right to keep it. I was so proud of it, and of him.

I told myself I could not think of it sold, to be handled by those who have no love for him. But he is King now, and much beloved by many. And still the ring stays with me, a symbol of my sin. For shame! I fidget in my chair, and Ursula hastens to ask, "Is there something you want, my lady?"

A clear conscience, I am tempted to reply, but why frighten her? "No, child, I am but impatient for the metal to be poured."

I little knew the making of a bell was so complex. It began with the arrival of Papion weeks ago. He consulted with me as to the size of the new bell, and sent for additional copper and tin to make up its new weight. He assayed them for purity and used the abbey wool scales to make sure he was getting the weight we were paying for.

Then he carefully selected a thick oak board, thicker at one end than the other. He made a cradle for it, and fastened a wooden crank to its thicker end. He made the shape of a bell in clay around the board, working slowly, layer upon layer, a few inches at a time. He said this represented the hollow inside the bell. The metal part he represented in tallow, pressing it into sheets between two boards and sealing the tallow onto the clay with a hot iron. Then he represented the air around the outside with more clay and enclosed the whole in iron hoops. He said his master, Roger Landon of Wokingham, taught him this method.

He brought an apprentice — whom he treats harshly — with him, and now has hired the blacksmith and four sturdy villeins from the village to assist him in this next portion of the process.

Pieces of the old bell mingle with copper ingots in the furnace, melting like ice in the springtime. Will the new bell sound a true note? The church bell in Deerfield sounds like someone beating on a pan with a wooden spoon. This bell will toll my passing and peal when my successor is chosen. I would like both to be pleasant sounds.

They will choose Sister Alys, we all know that. She is good, good to the point of saintliness, but she is also very sentimental. If I don't get rid of this ring, she will have it buried with me, and its weight will keep my soul from mounting to heaven. I tried to tell her that one time, but she said the soul was immaterial, so how could a material object weigh it down? But she saw my distress and comforted me by promising to sell the ring to pay for my brass.[lxiv] But I know her; she will slip that ring onto my finger before she puts me into the floor before the altar, the kind fool. I must not allow that to happen.

Lady Julia, who was abbess when I came to Deer Abbey, was also kind and sentimental, one of the most gentle and loving persons ever to carry a crozier. When Sister Agnes, Novice Mistress, complained she had caught me swinging on a rope in the great barn — I was five — Lady Julia only smiled and remarked that if God were displeased by my behavior, it would have been a simple matter for Him to have arranged for me to break my neck.

I climbed laboriously upwards, encouraged by the other children, and stood teetering on a high beam, the rough rope in my hands, testing my courage. Then, a lick of the lips and a step off into space, grip tightening, to swoop out, down — grin spreading — across, and up, turning at the end to face the ride back and down, letting go at the bottom to land breathless in a heap of fragrant hay.

"Is she asleep?" asks Austin.

"Yes, poor thing," says Ursula.

"No, I'm not!" I say crossly. I am not a 'poor thing!' But oh, to be young again, just for an hour, to soar on that rope once more! Lady Julia died the winter I was seven, and was succeeded by Lady

Tecla, who was the daughter of a Bavarian Duchess. She put me to my books (and oh, how I wept while I mastered the ugly black marks and made them speak to me!). Strange to think how I hated learning; one would not know the book-hungry young nun I became from the stubbornly illiterate child I was. I pray for her soul at every Mass, though I used to be terrified of her.

Everyone was frightened of her. Lady Tecla was a terrifying woman, easily provoked to rage, unrelenting in her demands for perfection, unafraid of anyone or anything. Doubtless the Sister Elizabeth described in the *Dialogus Miraculorum* was very like her.[lxv] I am sure I would cower if I saw the devil and be grateful to have merely the strength to sign myself with the cross. But my conscience is not so clear as Tecla and Elizabeth's.

For all it is a sunny day, I feel a sudden chill, and I lean gratefully toward the heat rising from Papion's oven. Papion is there, checking it again.

"Is it ready yet?" I ask

"Nay, we're still some way from pouring," he replies.

"It will be time for dinner soon," says Ursula. "Do you wish to return to the cloister, m'lady?"

I consider this. Sister Alys, who is cellarer, took Chapter for me this morning, a practice I have allowed more and more frequently of late, as the wrangles that arise at Chapter meetings discompose me. She is perfectly capable of seeing to the rest of the routine as well; there is no need for me to go back. And if I do, there will be the fuss of getting me safely back across the road, up the slope to the inner gate, across to the cloister, and into the misericord — and the equal fuss of getting me back again. "No, leave me be," I say, and lie, "I'm not the least hungry anyway."

Ursula and Austin confer briefly and Austin runs off toward the abbey, doubtless to tell them I am not returning just yet.

Maundy Thursday I washed the feet of as many poor as I had years, and we feasted on baked eels, rice, almonds and wine.

Austin is a fine man, capable and hard-working. He is only of medium height, but slim, all arms and legs, and so looks tall. He has a thick mop of curly brown hair and bright brown eyes, but his face is a bit too broad and his nose too short, reflecting his low birth. Freemantle chose him to be his assistant though Austin was barely fourteen, and never had cause to regret his decision. He must be in his forties now.

I remember the original John Freemantle when he first came to us, in fine but sorely used clothes and with not-quite-gentle manners. Even then he had an air of command, very comforting to a new abbess frightened at her lack of ability. He collected overdue rents, dealt with opportunate merchants, bargained for good rams to improve our flocks, threw our dishonest miller bodily into his pond, and persuaded the de Cynegils to show proper respect and courtesy to the new abbess, despite their disappointment at her choice. I learned to listen for his step and to take pleasure in his smile. I didn't realize what a danger he was to me until he married, and my bright resentment of his bride burned until Father Hugh spoke sharply to me of it and I ran to the confessional, enlightened and horrified. *Mea culpa, mea culpa, mea maxima culpa*[lxvi]...

Father Hugh often surprised me with his insight. Sister Harley, for example. I thought I was the only one who knew her well, but Father Hugh knew I was grooming her to succeed me. We had become very close, when she died abruptly nine years ago last Christmas. I fear I spoke sharply to God about that. But He wanted her, I suppose, and she fled to him, as we all should. Apoplexy, Lucas Barber said. Lucas fancies himself a doctor, though some of us can remember when he was a mere surgeon, and a beggar besides! She was outwardly proud but inwardly gentle and kind. Apoplexy, indeed.

I asked Father Hugh once if he tired of hearing me in the confessional, and he smiled and said it was like being stoned with cooked rice, most of the time. Though there was an occasional pebble, even the rare boulder, I think.

I miss Father Hugh. Father Edward is a fine priest, and he looks very priestly with his long narrow face and long narrow hands and his high, nasal voice. Father Hugh had none of those attributes ...

He was such a little man, we giggled up our sleeves at the sight of him. We called him our fool, and the abbey dwarf. Lady Tecla, still abbess, was barely civil to him. But he seemed utterly unaware of our rudeness, and was polite in all his dealings, competent in all his doings, going about his priestly business so serenely we began to be ashamed of ourselves. He proved to be stern with sinners but compassionate to the penitent. He was NOT a saint, for he loved some things of this earth too much: his little donkey, for example, and hot buttered scones, his funny old armor and racy gossip.

There are people who come all the way from Oxford and Banbury to visit his tomb now, and there are tales of miracles. Fools! He once confessed to me that he was terrified of making a mistake at the Consecration[lxvii], so how could he be a saint?

I remember, Lady Tecla and I saw him going out the postern gate one spring day after Sext with a long pole over his shoulder. "Whither, Priest?" she asked him in her coolest voice.

"To manual labor, Lady," he replied. "Old Taffy says there are some fine tench in Deer River."

"Surely that is an unseemly occupation for a priest?"

Father Hugh replied stoutly, "Our Lord selected fishermen to be his Apostles. And surely they who provide our Friday food are not to be scorned as unworthy."

"Humph!" she said, but let him go.

I told some others — Sister Eustachia, Sister Alys, the new novice Mildred — and we slipped out the postern gate to watch him when we had finished with our daily tasks, thinking to tease him. We were all young and irresponsible as sparrows.

Father Hugh saw us, called us over and showed us the fine bone hooks Old Taffy had given him, and explained how one judged the ripples in the stream to find the right place to drop the line. Interested now, we forgot about our plan to tease and watched him bait his hook, toss it out and work it downstream to just the right place. Sure enough, the tip of his pole bobbed, then bent sharply. How excited we were as he worked the struggling fish close to the shore, careful lest it break his line or wriggle off the hook. Finally it tired, and having guided it close in, he bent, thrust two fingers into its gills and lifted his catch, a large, desperately-wriggling tench! We marveled at his skill, and he accepted our compliments with a pleased air.

He put the fish in a basket, re-baited, and dropped his line back into the water. There was no immediate taker this time, and he bade us speak in hushed tones as perhaps our loud talk had frightened the fish. The waiting was pleasant, standing beside the gurgling river, listening to the song of birds, the cries of sheep, the merry whistle of a villein on the road. And soon there was another fish to keep the first company.

We petitioned Lady Tecla at Chapter the next morning to be allowed to learn the secrets of fishing from Father Hugh. She smiled that frosty smile of hers and assented, saying not all of us could control our desire to dabble in low, worldly things, and that any fish we caught were to be sent to the kitchen for next day's dinner.

We caught two fish apiece that day and set off a flurry of excitement among the other nuns — I fear we boasted somewhat of our accomplishments. The prospect of being at once idle and busy was not lost on them. By week's end, all but Lady Tecla were standing on the riverbank, dangling lines in the mysterious depths of the water; and Father Hugh was kept busy trotting up and down, exhorting us to silence, untangling our lines and baiting our hooks — for none but Mildred could bring herself to touch a worm. On Friday Lady Tecla came out to watch, with Thomas Camberwell, then our Steward, in close attendance. After a few minutes she borrowed a pole from Father Hugh and imperiously ordered us to clear a space for her at the bank. Father Hugh was directed to fasten his finest worm to the bone hook. Thomas tossed the line in for her, and then was ordered out of her way. A fish promptly took the bait and she lifted her pole high to pull him out of the water. The fish swung out and then in, to smack her solidly in the chest and spoil the pleats in her wimple. She dropped the pole with a shriek and stumbled back to sit heavily in some mud. Thomas rushed forward to help her while Father Hugh grabbed the pole, rescuing the fish. Unfortunately, I began to giggle. Equally unfortunately, everyone but Thomas joined in — except Father Hugh, but he had a look on his face that on reflection seemed neither humble nor Christian. That, of course, was the end of the fishing experiment, and all of us, including Father Hugh, had to beg her pardon the next day at Chapter.

But despite his common background, he had a subtle mind. I recall him telling me this little story: A famous usurer in Dijon came to be wed at church door, and during the ceremony a statue of God at the Last Judgment fell and killed him. All the other usurers in Dijon were frightened, of course, and they immediately took up a collection with which they bribed the priest to remove the rest of the statues from above the door.[lxviii]

I had been complaining to him about my problems with Edward of Oxford, whom I allowed Sister Harley to hire when her tasks as Bailiff seemed beyond her. "I have scolded him, I have scolded her," I said, "but he still flirts with my novices, snubs my nuns and plays one obedientiary against the other. I am at my wits' end." And Father Hugh nodded in agreement, then told the story. I thought he was changing the subject, but on reflection I saw I was no wiser than the usurers of

Dijon. I sent Edward of Oxford away, and when Sister Harley objected that she could not keep her books without him, I removed her from her post until she showed me she had acquired the necessary skills — which she did in gratifyingly short order.

Sometimes, when I am again at my wits' end, I think of him, and pretend I hear him telling me what to do. His advice remains good.

His armor, too small for anyone else to wear, and in any case severely damaged, is in a chest in my room. I dare not sell it; people would buy pieces of it and keep them as holy relics, which would bring the wrath of the bishop down on me. He is even more convinced than I that Father Hugh was no saint. As it is, villagers slip into the cloister on various pretenses and visit his grave, and they tell the chance traveler tales of miracles that happen when his name is invoked.

Once, when I was nine, I heard a tale and took it to the novice mistress. "Is it true, domina," I asked, "that Peter des Roches, Bishop of Rochester, could open his hand at any season of the year and release a butterfly?"[lxix]

"Yes, Margaret."

I said doubtfully, having heard quite the opposite, " Then surely he was a saint! How did he come by that power?"

She said, smiling, " He was hunting in the forest and had a vision of King Arthur in which the king invited him to a great feast, and this gift was given to him as proof his vision was a true one."

"Did this vision happen before he became a priest?"

"No, it was after."

"But priests ought not to hunt!" I said. "And he was a bad man in other ways, too. Then why was it granted he could do this miracle?"

"To show that miracles are no proof of holiness. They are among the proofs, but not the sole proof."

What's this? Ursula is holding a bowl under my nose. Nice smell. It is a sop of bread and chicken broth, brought from the kitchen for me. "I'm not hungry," I say.

But she says I must eat or I will be ill, and she nags until, for the sake of peace I agree.

We recite Grace. She hands me a spoon and holds the bowl while I eat a little. It is a delicious herbed broth, but I am minded that the Holy Rule commands Benedictines who are on short journeys from their abbey not to eat while away, and so eat only enough to satisfy her.

After lunch she, Papion, Austin and I recite the prayers and Psalm of Sext: "Thou art my God, and I will give thanks to Thee; Thou art my God, I will extol thee."

Then, "Papion, how goes it?" I ask.

"Well, my lady."

Good. I am growing tired.

How goes Deer Abbey? Have I been a good abbess? There were times when I tried my best and others when I was content to do barely enough. I turned out half the villeins at Broughton when we needed more pasture for our sheep, but I ignored gross shortages in the tithes offered by the rest when times were hard. Weighed in the balance, would I be found wanting?

Why do I concern myself with such questions? I am not finished being abbess yet.

Tomorrow or day after I must order the villeins into the fields, to gather our wheat and rye into shocks and stack them to dry. The peas are already gathered and covered against predacious birds. Then there is fall plowing, and the sowing of winter wheat. Perhaps after Christmas there will be time to look back. No, then there will be the regimen of Lent to prepare for. And after Easter tide, Herbfair to plan. We earned five shillings tuppence this year from entrance tolls, rent of booths and the sale of herbs and honey. Freemantle will be proud of us.

Not every abbess of every abbey has been good. I remember ... Lady Josiana Hohnsfal came to Deer Abbey when I was twenty-three, having been deprived of her office of abbess. She was a pale, cold, haughty lady, and rarely unbent enough to speak to any of us. With her came sad-faced Sister Ann, also sent from Minchon Abbey, who likewise seldom spoke to anyone. It was all mysterious and exciting.

But before six months had passed, our abbey was in turmoil. Nun spoke and acted against nun, cliques grew like poison mushrooms, and servants were giving notice in tears. None could explain it, but it had started when these two arrived, and our inclination was to see Sister Ann as the troublemaker: Lady Josiana had hinted at Ann's dark past.

Lady Josiana garnered for herself a private room in which she dined in state under the care of three servants, privileges not even our abbess had. Rumor had it she was related to the Queen's sister's husband, that Bishop Paul was a personal friend, that she had been illegally pushed from her former position by jealous rivals who would be discovered and punished. We basked in her rare approving looks and trembled at her snubs.

Meanwhile, Sister Ann did not eat enough to stay healthy and would not say what evil she had done to warrant so harsh a penance. Father Hugh, of course, warned us about judging not, and he was added to Josiana's list of people not spoken to. I spoke to Father Hugh anyway, but not to Sister Ann.

Tensions grew and tempers shortened beyond endurance, then Lady Elizabeth de Moran, our abbess, received a long letter from Bishop Paul, apparently in response to one she sent. I remember the day. Lady Josiana was summoned, and became hysterical. As farmerer, I was sent for. I tried to calm her but could not.

I called for Father Hugh, and stood by while he talked gently to her. At last he reached for her hand, but she yanked it back and struck him in the face, almost knocking him over. He rebuked her firmly, and she laughed, a cruel sound, but I thought it meant the worst was over. The laughter grew loud and horrible — and she began to choke. Her face turned blue, and she clawed at her throat as if to pull away invisible fingers. Father Hugh raised his hand in a blessing — we were both frightened — and she fell in a heap at his feet, stone dead. (Rumors of this occurrence now add color to villein tales of Father Hugh's supposed saintliness. He asked me not to speak of it, and I don't.)

She died unshriven. She had refused to take the sacraments from Father Hugh, and had sent to her family for her own priest. He had yet to arrive when this happened. She was buried in a lonesome corner of our graveyard. When I became abbess, I found the letter from Bishop Paul and read the true story of Lady Josiana.[lxx]

Immediately on her election as abbess of Minchon she sent for her mother and a pack of her relatives, who came for a visit and never left. Her brother was allowed to graze his cattle on abbey land. Her mother carried keys to abbey chests, and borrowed money which she never repaid. Josiana refused to make an annual account of income and expenses, and she never consulted with her nuns about expenditures. She provoked quarrels and played favorites. If she came late to Matins or Prime — which she did often — she made them stop and begin again. She sold the abbey's set of silver spoons for a quarter of their value, and kept for herself money willed to the abbey by a woman requesting prayers for her soul.

Near to the last straw, she took her steward, Thomas Camberwell, into her confidence, treating him to meals in her room and entertaining him far into the night. This encouraged others of her number to incontinence, knowing Josiana dared not rebuke them for fear her own actions would be reported in rebuttal. But in due time, one of her nuns, after two agonizing days of travail, produced a healthy baby girl. This fact was reported abroad by Lady Josiana's relatives, whose tongues ever ran on wheels about abbey affairs, and a week later the abbey was instructed to prepare for a visit from the bishop.

Bishop Paul, a good man as bishops go, was shown the baby. He took it from the mother and sent it away, and for penance had Sister Ann lead a procession around the cloister, unveiled and wearing white flannel, and ordered that she was to have no meat at any meal for a year, and on Fridays only bread and ale.

Still, Lady Josiana might have retained her post, had she not castigated poor Sister Ann that shameful day even more loudly than the bishop. Before he left, Bishop Paul gathered the nuns in their chapter house and inquired if there were other irregularities at Minchon. It is customary for nuns to reply to this question, "*Omnia Bene*." But this time, all was not well. First the cellarer, then two novices, then all of them began, each more eagerly than the last, to tell what they knew of Josiana. As soon as he realized the extent of their charges, Paul sent everyone out of the chapter house and brought them back one by one to see if their stories meshed and agreed. They did.

Then he called Josiana in. She told the bishop her nuns were jealous, spiteful wretches, given to lying and harlotry. She denied incontinence with her steward. She acknowledged not making an annual report or consulting with her nuns before making decisions, but said they were incapable of understanding such matters. She said her brother paid money for the privilege of grazing his sheep in abbey pastures. She said the spoons were not sold but merely mislaid. But Paul was doubtful, and said he would give her a week to produce four compurgesses to support her denial of the charges. Despite threats, exhortations and finally tears, she couldn't find even one.

Josiana was deposed and sent to us, whom the bishop considered a strong abbey in good order. Sister Ann requested a transfer, and was peremptorily ordered to accompany Josiana. When I did a history of Deer Abbey, I tiptoed carefully around Josiana. Now I would put boldly on paper what was done and said during that sad time, as a lesson to others.

Sister Ann lived to be fifty and never spoke of her actions, in sorrow or otherwise. In fact, she appeared indifferent to everything. Father Hugh advised me, after I became abbess, to treat her with special kindness, and I tried, though not very hard. She did not respond.

I remember going to see her on her deathbed. Oddly, she was almost cheerful and quite talkative. She told me she had dreamed she died and had gone to Purgatory, where she met a knight who had vowed to go on pilgrimage to the Holy Land and then not kept his vow. Now, every night, he is put down on the road to Jerusalem, taking up where he left off the night before. When he reaches his goal, she was told, he will be freed from the daytime flames.[lxxi] I suggested that perhaps her penance might be having to rise and suckle her babe every night while in Purgatory.

"No," she replied softly. "Surely there is no such joy in Purgatory."

Perhaps I should have tried harder with her. Our next abbess after Elizabeth was Lady Eleanor, who immediately ordered our cowshed re-roofed. It had partly burned a year before, but Elizabeth did nothing and in consequence three calves died of the damp. The re-roofing went very well; there was even pledge money left over. So Eleanor decided the dorter should have a new roof, and then that its windows should be glazed. These projects went well, but did not quite recover their expenses. (They would have, but for the failure of the executors of the will of Richard Stanton to send us the eleven pounds he left us — but as the proverb goes, two executors and an overseer make three thieves!)

Lady Eleanor licensed a glib-voiced man to go about garnering funds[lxxii] and embarked on building a magnificent guesthouse, with room to sleep twenty or more, with its own kitchen, a great hall larger than our church, a solar in the main guest room and its every window glazed. Before it was finished, she ordered a new malthouse with a dovecote over it, then added a fireplace to the kitchen, and another to her private quarters. She slated the priest's house roof and enlarged the stables. We spent the years of her rule in a glory of noise and sawdust.

She also left the abbey two hundred and twenty pounds in debt, a debt I inherited when I became abbess.

"But I thank God and ever shall, it was the sheep who paid for all," as the rhyme goes — with John Freemantle's help, of course. This bell is the only new thing I will bring to Deer Abbey, and even it is more by way of repair than genuinely new, as we are adding only twenty-five pounds of metal to the old bell in recasting it.

I did expand the herb garden. How I loved working in it! My hands and clothes smelled wonderful the whole time I was farmerer, whether I was setting out rows of comfrey or sage, or mixing simples in the still room. The fragrant smell, the esoteric knowledge gained, the relief brought to sufferers and — oh, yes, I will confess it — the respect given to one who moves knowledgeably in such areas, all were very satisfying.

Decoctions are easy to make and usually effective. They are used to clear the passages of the stomach, bowels, kidneys and bladder. You may keep a decoction a week unless the weather is hot. Decoctions made with wine last longer than if made with water. A decoction made of acorns and oak bark, in milk, will stop the bleeding of an ulcerated bladder. To clear the lungs, now, one uses an electuary, one made of clarified honey and nettle juice. For an old wound that remains moist, there is an ointment made of daisy leaves, animal fat, turpentine and beeswax that is very effective in drying and speeding healing.[lxxiii]

I remember being startled at how many recipes there are for bringing on a woman's courses, until our cook's daughter came to me asking for one, and I discovered soon after why she needed it.

I had just been named farmerer, and I was in the infirmary directing a thorough clean-out, when she came to me. I very proudly prepared the mixture, a decoction of nettle tops in wine, but she came back two days later saying it had not worked. The next, stronger, decoction made her very ill, and at that point Father Hugh intervened. Soon after there was a wedding and five months after that a healthy babe. I very carefully inquired into requests for such medicines thereafter.

I was never a novice mistress, having small patience with children. But novices can at least be guided into the quiet ways of abbey life. School children cannot. I never approved of the practice of taking in lay children, particularly boys. We did it frequently before I became abbess and they will doubtless resurrect the practice when I am gone. They may increase an abbey's income — if the parents are scrupulous about paying their fees — but their chatter and the tendency of the nuns to make pets of them is a distraction to the serenity, discipline and prayerful routine of an abbey. Our current bishop approves of the practice, but restricts it, allowing girl children only to the age of twelve and boys only to the age of nine. Others allow girls up to fourteen and boys up to twelve, which is ridiculous.

I recall a time when we were very poor, and agreed to take in a child in order to generate a mark or two of income. Little Katherine Wilton, whose father was somewhere in France, came to us when I was about nine. She was ten or eleven, and very shy. She brought no money or clothing with her, and all petitionary letters to her new stepmother brought sweet replies and no substance. Poor Katherine, who continued to grow despite what little food we could spare, was soon reduced to ill-fitting rags.

Finally, a trusted servant of her father was found to be in the neighborhood and he was invited to visit. He was shown the child, who was otherwise literate and well-mannered, and he went away thoughtful. Three weeks later he returned with an angry letter from Katherine's father, money to pay all her fees to date, and instructions to outfit her with a wardrobe befitting her station, which was also paid for. Our abbess composed a careful reply, in which, surrounded by all the courteous words at her command, she reminded him that it was not we who neglected the child, but her stepmother, and, less directly, himself. (I found a draft of the letter, full of respectful interlineations, in a chest of correspondence after I became abbess.)

Soon after, Katherine was removed to the care of a good family living near Chester. She was by then nearly thirteen, too old to be left in the care of gentle virgins, since she was to marry. I wonder what became of her? I wonder what her father did to her stepmother when he came home?[lxxiv]

"Look, a traveler!" says Austin, breaking into my musings "He's riding very hard."

"I see nothing," I say crossly, looking into the distance.

"I see him," says Ursula, rising onto her toes. "Coming down Broughton Road. There, he's gone out of sight at the bottom."

"He'll kill his horse if he keeps to that pace," says Austin. "What's he doing out on the road alone?" asks Ursula, who adds in a concerned tone, "And why is he being so cruel to his horse?" She has a tender heart.

"He'll be here in a while; we can ask him if he slows down," says Austin, smiling.

Ursula is a sweet child; in her case, lameness makes her aware of others' pain rather than centering her on her own. I hope she is as happy with us as we are with her.

Deer Abbey has mostly been fortunate in its nuns, at least during my lifetime — which has been a very long one. Abbeys must always be careful whom they admit. Bishops' recommendations, though they be necessary, are themselves often hedged about with "so I believe," and "as I am told." A tiny household of women, living so close-knit from one end of a year to another, is very susceptible to troublemakers. This goes not only for would-be nuns seeking admission, but people who wish to come and live as lay folk in an abbey "for the good of their souls." Often, this good they are seeking is something they have avoided all their lives — and they won't find us able to impose it on them, for we are human, too.

I recall a boisterous Chapter meeting at which a letter from the bishop was read, ordering us to admit Alice Northlede as a novice. She was already nearly twenty-five, he admitted, and strong-willed. That brought suppressed giggles. Alice lived with an uncle in Banbury and tales of his futile attempts to tame her or persuade her to marry had traveled even over our walls. We told the bishop, No thank you. However, a year later he tried again, and this time the dower offered was much higher — her uncle was growing desperate. Since we were at that time most anxious to find the funds to support our abbess' building program, we accepted her.

She sailed through her novitiate without difficulty; she was a bright young woman, if not handsome, and perhaps chastened by this strong action on her uncle's part. But it was this same Alice who, a year later, brought dishonor to the abbey by running off with a chance guest, a harper by trade, and living with him at Newcastle on Tyne for a few months. He doubtless found her as difficult as her uncle had, and she came back to us when he began beating her.

Her bruises soon healed, and pleasanter memories took their place in her mind; and she used to regale us with stories of life in a bustling city. We enjoyed the tales but agreed she would doubtless soon cause fresh scandal by running away again. Before we could prove our theory, she was carried off in the same outbreak of plague that took our abbess, two other nuns, our steward and our gardener.

Another exciting story-teller was, and is, Lucas Barber, whose tales of battle and bloodshed kept many of my younger nuns wakeful or nightmarish until I bid him cease frightening them. He is a biddable man, and thereafter he shared his stories only with the menfolk. But for all his exciting stories, I have never heard from him any expression of restlessness or regret at finding this safe harbor.

Not that abbeys are strangers to violence. A fierce battle was fought in the meadows beside the nunnery outside Northampton in 1460, and many of the slain are buried in its churchyard. And, of course, there was that terrible night when Fitzralph and his men came to cover their outrage of Lady Bertille by murdering her right in our church — killing Father Hugh when he stood in their way.

I should not have sent Bertille's daughter after Fitzralph. This is my biggest sin, for I deliberately aimed her at him, compounded her hurt and fury with well-chosen words, and almost destroyed her in my eagerness to get vengeance. *Mea maxima culpa* ....

"Why are you weeping, my lady?"

It is Ursula. "Nothing, child, just the tears of a weak, old woman." How often have I heard those same words from elderly nuns? And believed them, even as Ursula believes me. The shadows lengthen; I want to go home. "Papion, how much longer?"

"Very soon now, m'lady." He is tired from his labors, having been at his tasks in the field since last night. "I am waiting now for the green flame," he adds.

"Green flame?"

"That will tell me the copper in the mix is — There! Now, everyone: Do as I told you! Quickly!" The bellows increase their rhythm, and a villein puts more charcoal on the fire. Papion comes to the place at my feet and skillfully begins removing the well-set stones with a pair of long-handled tongs. Austin picks up another pair from a heap of earth and begins to help him. The stones are tossed aside quickly. The last one is still rolling when the tongs are dropped and shovels picked up to fill in the hole again. Austin shovels, but another workman takes Papion's place at the task of filling the pit.

"What are you doing?" I ask. "You haven't poured the metal yet!" Two villeins with blunted wooden poles come to tamp down the dirt as it is shoveled in.

Papion, shoveling frantically, gasps an explanation: "The mold would break from the weight of the metal were it not supported by the earth."

At last the pit is nearly filled, only the top of the mold showing, and the shovels are put down. Papion hurries back to his fire, and stirs it with a blackened stick.[lxxv] Now more metal, tin this time, is added, and the mixture stirred as thoroughly as if it were a fine sauce in our kitchen. Soon now, soon the metal will be poured. I feel a little giddy; it is the heat, or perhaps I am hungry. And surely it is only excitement that makes my breath come fast.

"Break down the fire!" orders Papion at last, and the charcoal is raked aside from the nearer fire. Long poles are thrust into the handles of the great pot, and two very stout villeins carefully hoist it and stagger to the mold with it. Ursula backs away to give them more room.

Papion puts a straining cloth across the top of the mold and, very carefully, the pot is tipped so that its molten contents begin to spill into it. Papion flings himself face down onto the ground to listen to the metal go into the mold. "Hold!" he calls and the men laboriously pull the pot back a little. "Go ahead," he orders, and they tip it forward again. Sweat is running down their faces, and their arms tremble with their effort.

After a while, "That's all there is, Pappy," says one of the workmen.

"Quick, take it away! Bring the other, quick, quick!" shouts Papion. His face is turned away from me, he is listening to the metal run down into the mold. Austin is helping rake the charcoal away from the other pot. Ursula is looking down the road for the rider. The workmen turn away with their burden, and swiftly, before anyone can see what I am about, I reach out and drop Richard's ring into the mold. The rising heat burns my hand and brushes my face like dry, old feathers from a long-dead wing.

The ring will quickly dissolve into the rest of the metal, and become one with the bell. When the bell is consecrated, so will this bit of gold be blessed. God save our noble King, I pray, and I am free of my burden at last.

The second pot is brought, and emptied in fits and starts into the mold. There seems to be a danger the metal will overflow, but after a moment, with a tiny gurgle, it settles out of sight, and there is exactly enough left in the pot to bring it up to the top again.

Suddenly all the hustle stops. "Is it finished?" I ask.

"Well, m'lady, yes and no," says Papion.

"What do you mean?" I ask.

"The metal is poured, the bell is cast. But now we must wait a little, then dig it out, raise it, and remove the inner mold. After a day or so we can remove the bell from its outer mold. Then I will file it smooth, hang it and tune it."

"No bless it first," I say, already thinking of the ceremony, which is more elaborate than the making of an abbess. The bell will be washed and anointed and censed and blessed, all under the supervision of a bishop. It will be named — bells have names, like people — and be a holy object, almost a Christian.

"Why dig it up?" I ask. "With all the metal, it's heavier now than it was before, and hot besides; why not just let it harden where it is?"

"Because the clay inside the bell swells as it cools, and it would break the metal. We'll do as we did to get the mold into the pit, lift one side a little and put earth under it, then left the other side and put earth under it, and so bring it up to the surface."

"It will be a good bell," I think.

"I have done all in my power to make it so, madame," he says — I must have spoken my thought. I smile at him. He turned out very well; he is one of my successes.

Ursula comes again to stand beside me. "You should not have leaned forward like that, my lady," she scolds, but quietly. "I feared you would fall."

"There was nothing to fear," I say, trying to discern in her face just how much she saw. "I hope you won't worry the others with the story of it."

She bends to tug my coverlet back into place and tucks my now-empty hand under it. "I will speak no more of it, all right?" she says. God bless the child!

"Look, here comes the traveler," says Austin, shading his eyes.

I can see him now, a dark shape on the pale road.

"His horse is tired," remarks Papion, but indifferently. He is watching the metal at the top of his mold, waiting for it to harden.

The tired horse forces the rider to slow. Or perhaps he is going to stop.

My chest feels tight. Have I been a good abbess? Why am I haunted by that question today? I have been an ordinary abbess, I suppose, I conclude crossly: autocratic at times, tender-hearted at others, charitable and vain, fearing God while loving the things of this world. The abbey is out of debt, my obedientiaries are capable, our harvest bids to be fair this year, the flocks are recovering from the decimation of murrain two years ago. The stable doors need replacing and there is a small leak in the cloister roof. Two villeins ran away, but they waited until after spring plowing, and one may return in time to help with the harvest.

I can see the rider more clearly now. He's a tall man, with a cloak flapping around the rump of his horse as he approaches. The horse is stumbling with weariness.

"IT'S JOHN FREEMANTLE!" shouts Austin, and he begins to run for the road.

Why, I believe it *is* young John! What would make him ride that hard? What news? Is something wrong? The tightness in my chest runs down my arm to my very fingers. I cannot stand.

Ursula is running with Austin to meet him, shouting greetings. The horse stops and Freemantle dismounts. Oh, what news of the King? A mighty victory, surely. I will sit back and calm myself, and wait for him to come to me.

They are talking and talking. Papion and his workers have gone to listen, and I am alone.

Alone and giddy, as I was that time on the ledge.

With the thick, rough rope in my hands, waiting for the courage to step forward.

I can smell the hot hay, hear faintly the encouraging words of the other children. The sun is shining so strongly through the cracks of the barn wall that it makes a dazzling light before my eyes. I already feel I am falling, I have but to yield to it. No, wait. I am afraid.

Look, there is Father Hugh! He is reaching out to me, he will catch me if I fall. Dear Father Hugh. What is he saying? Oh, of course: *In manus tuas* ...
lxxvi

Excerpt From a Late-Victorian Survey of Cotswold Villageslxxvii

Near the village of Deerfield on the Broughton Road lie the ruins of an ancient monastery. The outer wall remains mostly intact, but the gatehouse is only fragmentary. With permission from the owner to explore the pasture, the visitor can trace the outline of the old cloister. Doe-eyed cows graze in and around the ruined walls of the church, and the barn is a very fine late example of an abbey guesthouse. What stories these stones could tell, of sweet, sad voices in the night raised in plaintive chant!

In Deerfield itself a quaint old church survives. In its square Norman tower hangs a bell dubbed Old Meg. It possesses a note of surpassing sweetness. Legend has it that Old Meg is the abbey bell, stolen from under the very noses of Henry VIII's men at the time of the dissolution. The author climbed the worn steps to the belfry and can attest that the bell, which appears to date from the late fifteenth century, has an inscription around its rim which reads, "Margaret made me: and let her works praise her." But who Margaret was, and why she made the bell, is lost to history.

Sources

First and foremost, of course, *Medieval English Nunneries, ca. 1275 to 1535,* by Eileen Power, Biblo and Tannen, New York, 1964. It was a limited edition, so if you find a copy (try a university library) you can have it photocopied without worrying about copyright infringement. It is fascinating reading.

Life in the Middle Ages, writings selected and translated by G. G. Coulton, and published by The MacMillan Company, Cambridge, England, in 1935. (Previous editions dating to 1910.) This is a priceless source for anyone wanting a peek at the beliefs and attitudes of medieval people. If I had to give up all but one of my reference works, it would kill me to choose between this and *Medieval English Nunneries.*

Theophilus, *On Divers Arts,* translated from the Latin by John G. Hawthorne and Cyril Stanley Smith. A Dover Publications paperback

Discovering Bells and Bellringing a small paperback by John Camp, Shire Publications, Ltd., printed and reprinted in 1968, 1971,1977, 1979, and 1981.

Macklin's Monumental Brasses, revised by John Page-Phillips, Frederick A. Praeger, Publishers. A surprisingly disappointing book insofar as illustrations go.

The English Abbey, by F. H. Crossley, F.S.A., 2nd Ed., revised, B. T. Batsford, Ltd., London (1935)

Monastic Life in Medieval England, by J. C. Dickinson, Barnes & Noble, Inc., New York (1962)

Military & Religious Life in the Middle Ages and the Renaissance, by Paul Lacroix, Frederick Ungar Publishing Co., New York (1874, reprinted 1964)

Medieval Women, by Eileen Power, Cambridge University Press, London (1975)

Medieval People, by Eileen Power, Barnes & Noble, Inc., New York (1963)

To the King's Taste, Richard II's book of feasts and recipes, adapted for modern cooking by Lorna J. Sass, The Metropolitan Museum of Art, New York (1975)

My Sunday Missal (Explained), by Rt. Rev. Msgr. Joseph F. Stedman, Confraternity of the Precious Blood, Brooklyn, NY (1949 printing)

A B C of Gothic Architecture, by John Henry Parker, C.B., 3rd Edition, Parker & Co., London (1882)

Shaftesbury and Its Abbey, by Laura Sydenham, The Oakwood Press, England (1959)

An Encyclopedia of World History, Ancient, Medieval, and Modern, Chronologically Arranged, compiled and edited by William L. Langer, Houghton Mifflin Co., Boston (1948)

Langland — *Piers the Ploughman*, translated into modern English by J. F. Goodridge, Penguin Books, Hunt Barnard & Co., Ltd., Aylesbury, England (1966)

Fifteenth Century England, by Percival Hunt, University of Pittsburgh Press (1962)

St. Joan of Arc, by Rev. Denis Lynch, S.J., Benziger Brothers, New York (1919)

Medieval England, A social history and archaeology from the Conquest to 1600 A.D., by Colin Platt, Charles Scribner's Sons, New York (1978)

The Great Schism, 1378, by John Holland Smith, Heybright and Talley, New York (1970)

Signs & Symbols in Christian Art, by George Ferguson, Oxford University Press, New York (1954, reprinted 1964

Bede, *A History of the English Church and People*, translated into modern English by Leo Sherley-Price, Penguin Classics, Penguin Books, Ltd., Middlesex, England; Baltimore, MD (1955)

The Little Breviary, containing in simplified form all the offices of the Roman Breviary, translated into English by Msgr. Ronald A. Knox, Sheed & Ward, Inc. New York (1950 printing)

English Lyrics Before 1500, edited by Theodore Silverstein, Northwestern University Press, Evanston, IL (1971)

The Book of Common Prayer, According to the use of the Protestant Episcopal Church in the United States of America (1945) for the 51st Psalm and Margaret's blessing of Eulie

The Holy Rule: Notes on St. Benedict's Legislation for Monks, by Hubert Van Zeller, Sheed & Ward, New York, 1958

Dr. William Delehanty, Chairperson, History Department, College of St. Thomas, St. Paul, MN

Dr. C. Winston Chrislock, History Department, College of St. Thomas, St. Paul, MN

Deacon Michael Stevens (to be ordained a Priest in May), St. Paul Seminary, St. Paul, MN, for the correct date of Easter in 1436

Rev. Carl Volz, instructor at Luther Seminary, St. Paul, for valuable information about the Mass in the Fifteenth Century

The cover illustration for *Thy Daily Bread* was drawn by Margaret Shaftesbury

The illustrations for *Deliver Us From Evil* and *Thy Will Be Done* were drawn by Christopher Huddle, whose persona inspired the character of Sir Christopher Huddleston.

Endnotes

i Vestments

The vestments a Catholic priest would wear while saying Mass in the Fifteenth Century do not differ significantly from the style set in the Eighth Century — or from what is worn in the Twentieth.

The *Amice* is a rectangle of white linen tied round the shoulders. It used to be a hood. It is taken as a symbol of the cloth used to blindfold Christ when He was crowned with thorns, and as an emblem of protection against evil thoughts.

Alb means white, and the *Alb* is a full-length white linen robe with long sleeves. It comes from the white tunic worn by Roman nobles. It symbolizes the purity of a priest's body and soul, required by his function. The alb is tied at the waist by a white rope knotted at the ends. This *Cincture* symbolizes the rope used to tie Jesus to the pillar for scourging, and also the restraint the priest puts on his passions.

The *Maniple* (*manus plena* = full hands) is a band of material worn on the left forearm. It once served as a kerchief to wipe away sweat and dust, and is a reminder that the priest is a worker. It symbolizes the manacles with which Christ was fastened when He was arrested.

The *Stole* is a long strip of cloth that goes around the neck, crossing on the breast, and reaching nearly to the floor on both sides. It is held in place by being tucked under the cincture. It is symbolic of the cross Jesus carried. Once a mark of authority, the stole is a reminder to the priest to uphold the dignity of his calling.

A circular cape of rich material, **the *Chasuble*** is often beautifully embroidered. It is marked on the back with a cross. It recalls the "seamless garment" legend says Mary wove for her Son and for which the soldiers on Calvary cast dice. It symbolizes the all-embracing yoke of service a priest takes on; that "My yoke is sweet" is signified by the richness and beauty of the garment.

The maniple, stole and chasuble come in sets of matching colors. *White* is symbolic of light, joy and purity, worn at Christmas and other happy feasts of Jesus, on feasts of the Virgin and on feasts of saints not martyred. *Red* is for blood and fire, and red vestments are worn on the feasts of martyrs and of the Holy Spirit. *Green*, for hope, is worn from Pentecost to Advent, from Epiphany to Lent. Penitential *purple* is worn during Lent and Advent. *Rose* is worn on the third Sunday of Advent and fourth Sunday of Lent.

ii **Obedientiaries**

The officers of an abbey, priory or monastery were called *obedientiaries*. The first in rank was the Abbot or Abbess, who was elected by the monks or nuns. He or she in turn named the other officers.

The *Abbess* was an absolute ruler. Although important matters were usually discussed in Chapter meetings, the final decision lay entirely in her hands. Royal abbeys had the election of the new Abbess confirmed by the king; ordinary abbeys by the Pope. (Confirmation was not always automatic.)

The *Cellarer* was usually second in command to the Abbess. She leased land and buildings, bought and sold property, appointed overseers with the approval of the Abbess, supervised all lay labor and was in charge of everything concerning food, drink, fires and granaries. Her aide, if she had one, took over charge of the kitchen, brewery and gardens.

The *Precentor* was chief singer, librarian and archivist. She was one of three (along with Abbess and Cellarer) having access to the Abbey Seal and keys to the chest in which important papers and valuables were kept. In big abbeys her aide, **the Succentor**, was responsible for keeping track of the population and poking sleepers awake in Church.

The *Sacrist* was in charge of the Church and its contents. Getting sacred vessels repaired, finding a carpenter or stone mason to repair the "fabric" (structure), making and repairing vestments, were all duties of the Sacrist. She also arranged ordinary funerals and set the fire watch.

The *Kitchener* was chief cook. She bought food not supplied by the abbey farms and gardens, and kept inventory of dishes and utensils. Once a month she made a detailed report of accounts.

The *Fraterer* was responsible for the frater, or dining hall. She made sure there were clean tablecloths and that worn ones were mended or replaced, that fresh rushes or straw was put on the frater floor. In the summer, she arranged for flowers, fennel and/or mint to be tossed into the air to sweeten it in the frater. She saw to it that the lavatory was kept clean, that there was warm water available, a whetstone and clean sand were in place to clean eating knives, and that there were enough clean towels.

The *Chamberlain* was in charge of everything domestic but food. Straw was changed annually in the mattresses, probably at the same time the dorter floor was thoroughly scrubbed. She arranged for the quarterly baths and for feet washing on Saturday nights. Linen was changed fortnightly on beds in the summer; every three weeks in winter. She arranged for a lamp or two in the dorter at night, and extinguished them when everyone was safe in bed.

The *Farmerer* took care of the infirmary. She made sure a lamp was burning all night long, and that special food was available as necessary. She consulted a physician if one were available and necessary, provided warm baths, draughts, "electuaries" and all things needed for the convalescent. She often planted and cared for an herb garden, from the products of which she brewed "simples," medicines for her patients. She arranged for Last Rites and comforted the dying.

The *Almoner* was the alms-giver. She visited the sick of her sex in a nearby town or village, if there was one, and provided care for sick lay people. She was in charge of security, of keeping the abbey free from intruders. It was her responsibility to see that "broken meats" and other leftovers from the frater made their way to the front gate of the abbey, to be distributed to the poor.

The *Hosteller* was responsible for the excellent care given to visitors. She entertained the guests, or arranged for entertainment, made sure everything from dry clothing to writing materials was on hand. She also was responsible for seeing that departing guests did not steal any towels.

The *Steward* may best be described as a "foreman." It is very likely that at all religious houses of women this position was filled by a man. He worked directly with the laborers and tenants of the abbey, under the supervision of the *Cellarer*.

The smaller the house, the more likely two or more of these positions would be filled by one person. Also, by the Fifteenth Century an abbey of well-bred ladies would be likely to hire a lay woman to be their chief cook, and fill at least some of their other obedientiaries' roles from a supervisory position.

iii **The Cloister**

Imagine a large square lawn, oriented to the compass. Surrounding the lawn on all four sides is a stone arcade of arches, the upper half of each arch filled with stained glass, and the whole roofed with lead. The outside of the arcade is fastened to a series of buildings which enclose the square. All of this — lawn, arcade, buildings — is the *Cloister*.

Taking up the north side of the cloister is the biggest and most important building: **the *Church***. Its head is to the east; a bell tower takes up the west end. The cloister lies to the south of the church to take advantage of the winter sun. The foundations of Deer Abbey's church are pre-Norman, but the church (the entire cloister, actually) was extensively rebuilt in the Decorated style early in the Fourteenth Century, thanks to a bequest from the will of Queen Eleanor (the Infanta de Castile), Edward I's wife.

Walking from east to west down the flagstone ***Cloister Walk,*** we note cabinets which hold books in current or daily use, three desks with tops shaped like inverted V's for the use of those writing letters or copying books (ink runs out of goose quills used on horizontal surfaces, and scrolls roll themselves up unless draped over something), and a door about a third of the way along that opens into the church. This is the widest of the four cloister walks, because it is the warmest, and it is here that the nuns copy books and manuscripts, spin, sew, or do some of the embroidery that has made *opus Anglicanum* (English work) famous all over Europe. At the west end of the walk an elaborate stone arch over a massive wooden door marks the entrance to the porch of the church.

The *Porch* is a small room with narrow windows and four doors. A set of doors on the right open into the small nave of the church. On the left are two doors. The nearer leads to the west cloister walk, the farther to narrow and worn stone steps that lead up to the dorter.

The *Dorter* is a long, exceedingly plain dormitory. The eleven simple beds do not begin to fill it; there is an open area at the far end. Thin, straw-filled pallets are on the beds. There are no tables, chairs or other furnishings in the hall. There is a low shelf by the door we have just come in by; it is just large enough to hold the small oil lamp that rests on it. Near the foot of each bed is a pair of boots made of sheep hides inside out. The nuns almost never see this room by daylight. At the far end of the dorter are two doors, one on the left and the other in the middle. The one on the left leads to the Abbess' quarters.

The middle doorway leads down some steps to **the *Reredorter***, sometimes called **the *necessarium***. It's a seven-holer, with little doorless booths for privacy of a sort. Deer Abbey, like most abbeys, has surprisingly advanced ideas of sanitation. A nearby stream (there was nearly always a stream — the site was picked with this in mind) was partly or wholly diverted into a culvert which fed into an underground stone-lined tunnel running under the south side of the cloister. It was a source of water for the kitchen and lavatory, and kitchen scraps could be fed into it at the downstream end before it rolled under the reredorter. (It was the discovery of these "secret tunnels" by people who still hadn't caught on to the causes of dysentery that led to all sorts of scandalous conjecture about the behavior of cloistered men and women.)

There is a door from the reredorter into **the Abbess' Quarters.** This used to be the infirmary for sick and aged nuns, but they now have a building outside the cloister, in the inner courtyard. Our view of the Abbess' quarters is nearly blocked by a tall and elaborately carved wooden screen. It is called the Virgin Screen because it has scenes from the life of the Virgin Mary, from her birth to wealthy parents to her coronation as Queen of Heaven. On this side of the screen is a narrow wooden bed identical to the ones in the dorter. It is covered by a smokey-hued blue woolen blanket whose edges touch the floor, and a large, hard-looking pillow. There is a large wooden chest which has seen better days at the foot of the bed.

On the other side of the screen is the rest of the large room, with its blue-tiled floor with a pattern of interlocking white rings bordered with heraldic white roses. There are three tapestries on the wall, one of the Nativity, one showing the taking down of Jesus from His cross, and one of a lady comforting a unicorn about to be slain by hunters. The fire in the fireplace is banked. To the left of the fireplace is a door leading out into a *Passageway* leading out of the cloister to the inner courtyard, an L-shaped area containing **the *Infirmary***, the two ***Guest-***

Houses (one is for poor and ordinary folk simply seeking a place for the night; the other is for the Bishop and Sir Richard and the traveling merchants) and the priest's house. There is an outer court that contains **the *Almonry*** and granary and stables and other buildings and the gate-house.

Across the passageway is **the *Kitchen*** block. The first part is called **the *Brewery***. Ale is made here every few days because it goes sour if it is kept. There is a whey-press in the corner; they make cheese here, too. The next area is **the *Bakehouse***, with ovens built into the sides of the enormous fireplaces. The tables are not so clean as we would like them. The next room is **the *Kitchen* proper**. It has pots and pans large and small, each with an assigned use, with knives, spoons and ladles all neatly put away or hanging from a nail. There are not a lot of utensils and most show some signs of repair. There are several little oil lamps scattered around the room, and a number of straw pallets shoved under a table shows people sleep here. Near a door leading into the cloister (there is another door leading into the frater) is a large cistern which holds warm water for the lavatory.

The *Lavatory* is outside, in the corner where the kitchen and frater meet. It is a marble pillar about five feet high, carved with fish and frogs and turtles. There are brass spigots bending out all around, each with its own stopcock — not unlike a faucet you might meet in an older home today. A catch basin circles the pillar. It has several drains for waste water. On top of the pillar is a jar of malodorous soap the consistency of library paste. There is clean white sand in a box for cleaning eating knives, and a small whetstone. There are clean linen towels on hooks on the walls.

The first building on the east walk of the cloister is **the *Frater***, or dining hall. There was always a painting of the Crucifixion on the wall at one end, under which was located the head table. Built into an adjacent wall, over the heads of the diners was **the *Pulpitum***, from which a different reader each week read something edifying in a slow, clear voice, repeating significant passages. A ***Misericord*** was supposed to be part of, or connected to, the frater, in which the very young, the aged or the recently-bled could get more nourishing meals than the ordinary fare. But by the Fifteenth Century it was not uncommon for everyone in the cloister to decide that the poor sort of diet ordered by the Rule was too difficult for them, and to have all meals served in the misericord.

North of the frater is **the *Warming Room***, also called the ***Calefactory***, or common room. It has a fire burning in it from All Saints (November 1) to Easter. Nuns could resort to this room for a few minutes to thaw out or, when clouds kept the sun from warming the cloister, simply spend the afternoon here working.

There is another *Passageway* or ***Slype*** between the warming room and chapter house. It leads to the orchard and cemetery. When the Rule of Silence is enforced, it is in this little alley that urgent conversations may be held.

Across the passageway from the warming room is **the *Chapter House***. It is of the characteristic multi-sided shape of abbey chapter houses. Daily meetings are held here to mete out punishments, thrash out problems affecting everyone and to handle the business of running the abbey. Most chapter houses, like this one, were located next to the church.

And so we have come back to where we started, at the eastern end of the north cloister walk.

iv   The inventory is adapted from the inventory of the nuns of Sheppey taken at the Dissolution of the Abbeys in the reign of Henry VIII (begun in 1536). Sheppey had more of everything, mostly, including 430 "wethers and lammys," 700 bearing ewes, 535 "twelvemonthyngs, ewes and wethers," and 560 ewes "in lambys."

v   Things "desmane" belong to the abbey directly, and the desmane sheep are the only ones to be shorn whose wool belongs entirely to Deer Abbey. Tenants may bring their sheep to Shearing Meadow and pay a percentage of the sale price the abbey negotiates to have their sheep shorn. Villeins must bring their sheep to be shorn and pay not only a percentage but a tithe as well.

A Word on Villeins: After the 13th century villeins were in a position like slavery with regard to their lords, though they had rights in relation to anyone else. They were bound to the land they lived on, and if the land was sold they went with it. Deer Abbey villeins belong, most of them, to South Broughton Manor, a piece of land separate from abbey land, with its own church and priest. The priest is paid a salary, and any income the church earns comes to Deer Abbey. Should the abbey sell its manor, villeins, church and priest (including the income) go with it.

vi   The Cotswold sheep as a breed still exists today, but because of improvements to other breeds, its wool is now considered "coarse." It is a white-faced animal whose surface wool lies in long curls about the diameter of a pencil.

vii   Taken from a very detailed account book of St. Radegund's, Cambridge, for the year 1449-50. (The fiscal year is older than you think.) Two tenements were to be built in "Nunneslane," next to the nuns' dwelling place. They were to be of clay and wattle, with stone foundations and thatched roofs. It is from accounts like this that a detailed picture of how these houses were built as well as their cost is given. According to Eileen Power, "The walls had to be filled between the beams with clay, strengthened with a mixture of reeds and sedge and bound with hemp firmly nailed to the beams." (The hemp and nails cost sixteen pence.)

viii   The cost given for the repair is again from St. Radegund's, for repair to a gutter between those same two tenements — since St. Radegund's had them built, unlike Lady Margaret! (Sure enough, one caught fire, though it did not burn to the ground, and sedge had to be bought to repair it.)

ix   Eileen Power noted, in *Cambridge Economic History*, a tendency on the part of villeins to buy land instead of freedom, apparently discounting the continued drag "boon work" and other duties could be. Some would even marry back into villeinage if thereby a bit more land could be acquired. (A villein could have land of his own, but if he was bound to any, he was still a villein. Land could be acquired through purchase or by clearing waste or draining marshland.) The standard price for a Charter of Manumission was eight marks, but many lords sold them for less — particularly if they wanted to clear the land of people to make room for sheep.

x   The Abbey of Wroxton bought a cow for its guesthouse for the price indicated.

xi   Quote from the *Holy Rule: Notes on St. Benedict's Legislation for Monks,* by Hubert van Zeller; and idea for commentary taken from the same. Benedictine nuns live under the same Rule the monks do.

xii   John and Thomas Fortey were real woolmen, members of the Staple, who lived and bought wool in the Cotswolds the latter part of the 15th century. John Fortey died in 1458 and his brass, as described in the story, is in Northleach Church in the Cotswold district. Thomas died in 1474 and his brass is near his father's.

xiii   William Breton, woolman and wool packer, bought a general pardon from the king in 1458. He was frequently hired by the Celys, whose letters about their doings in the wool trade survive to this day. Breton was twice involved in illegal wool packing for Lombards.

xiv   I could not find the name of an honest wool packer, so I made up the name of John Byford.

xv   The terms proposed by Fortey are by far the usual ones. The better ones Lady Margaret insists on keeping (precedent counted for a great deal in the Middle Ages) could be gotten.

xvi   There was a great deal of ill feeling on the part of English woolmen about the Lombards — or any foreigner dealing in English wool. The Staple had 300 members and was a monopoly, controlling 4/5 of English wool exported. Like all monopolies, it was unhappy about the small share outside its control. In the year 1273 there were 32,743 sacks of wool exported (sack = 364 lb.). In 1470-71 it had dropped considerably, but was still over 9,900 sacks. (This was due, I believe, to the rise in domestic cloth making.) A poem called *Libelle of Englyshe Poylcye* described "in verse more remarkable for economic enthusiasm than for poetic fire" (Eileen Power) the beauty of English wool and the nastiness of the Lombard. It is from this poem that Thomas Fortey gets his description of the Lombard's behavior and his quote at the end.

Because of the size of the wool trade, the customs and subsidies paid by exporters made up a substantial part of the income of the crown. Kings would sometimes borrow money from the Staple, using expected income as collateral. None of the Plantagenets were good managers, and as a consequence, by 1464 the crown owed the Staple 32,861 pounds. In an attempt to get out from under, the king made the head of the Staple (called the Mayor) Treasurer and Surveyor of the Works of Calais. He and his Lieutenant were to collect all customs and subsidies and out of them pay the wages of the garrison at Calais, the Tower of Tysbank and the castles of Guinnes and Hammes, and to maintain their fortifications — and take 3,000 pounds themselves until the debt was paid. They were also to pay for the twice-annual convoy of the wool fleet to Calais among other expense and if there was anything left over (!) the surplus was to go to the royal treasury. It was estimated that disbursements by the Staple to meet this arrangement for one year would be 15,022 pounds, 4 shillings, 8 pence.

xvii   In the late 1400's, an alien would pay 53 shillings, 4 pence in customs and subsidies on one sack of wool. An English woolman would pay 40 shillings. (Or he could smuggle — an English abbot was once accused of smuggling — and hope an irate and powerful Staple, or equally irate and even *more* powerful king, did not catch him.) The king himself, either directly or through agents, engaged in the sale of wool.

xviii   There is no St. Geoffrey. This is a medieval way of saying, "Don't hold your breath, honey."

xix   Cade is an old word for pet, especially an animal raised by hand. Jack Cade led a popular uprising in 1450, so calling a cade lamb Jack in 1454 seems natural enough.

xx   If anyone should find this story too romantic to take seriously, he or she should dip some time into the Paston letters for a true 15th century story of a woman who wanted to marry a family servant and the severe (and unsuccessful) measures they took to dissuade her. See *The Pastons and Their England* (H. S. Bennett, Cambridge University Press), chapter 5; or from Letter No. 607 in a collection of them. Trothplight was absolutely binding, as serious and permanent a step as marriage.

xxi   Free warren was the right to take small game in and around a royal forest.

xxii   In those terrible days before anesthetic, the idea was to perform an operation as quickly as possible, to get in and out before the patient died of shock. There is a record of a surgeon removing an assistants fingers during the amputation of a patient's leg. There were probably fragments of spinach pie on and about Father Hugh before the pie was in five parts.

xxiii   To be easily moved to tears was a gentle quality highly prized in the Middle Ages, even among the toughest fighting knights.

xxiv   I doubt very much if the herriot argument would have held water in the case of Jamie. Promising villein children were taught their letters by their Parish priest. If further education appeared helpful, a patron was sought to pay for time at a university. Students there had to take some degree of Holy Orders, and the next step for the villein would be the priesthood. The Church was willing to overlook low birth in brilliant priests, and the patron might find himself rewarded with a close, and obligated, friend high in influence at court (the Church had its say in the King's Council). So, while it is possible that Deer Abbey would take in and teach a villein child his letters (especially if it was running a school for youngsters of nobility anyway), it is more likely that Jamie would be left to the tender mercies of Father John Isling's successor.

xxv   Words and pebbles make up an old Saxon charm. I think it is the pebbles that do the trick.

xxvi   This claim for skill in grafting — an impossible one — was often made. Medieval people enjoyed experiments in grafting.

xxvii   Richard II was deposed (in 1399) and murdered by his cousin, the Duke of Lancaster, who became Henry IV. Henry VI was his grandson. If Richard II was the last true king, then, by some people's reckoning, the Duke of York was his true heir. (Now you know the cause of the War of the Roses. Lancaster was red, York white.)

xxviii   Murrey (mulberry, a dark red) and white were the colors of the House of York.

(Lancaster wore blue and white.) Virtually everything this man does and says over the first two pages of this story matches historical descriptions of him.

xxix   Terce is about 9:00 a.m. The canonical hours and their approximate times (they varied with the season to keep them somewhat equidistant) are: Matins and Lauds, Midnight; Prime, dawn or 6:00 a.m. Terce, 9:00 a.m.; Sext, 12:00 noon; None, 3:00 p.m. (although this slowly crept earlier until it gave its name to midday, pushing the morning hours together); Vespers, sunset or 6:00 p.m.; Compline, bedtime, 8-9:00 p.m. Non-clerical folk were familiar with these terms and their meaning, and used the ringing of church bells to mark the passage of their own day.

xxx   Tally sticks, cut with notches, were the way a largely illiterate population kept track of the numbers of things. The size of the notches indicated whether the numbers were in ones, tens, hundreds or even thousands (the last a notch the size of the edge of a man's hand). (*Encyclopedia Britannica* of 1945)

xxxi   A ring matching this description was found at Bosworth Field in 1485. He apparently had a number made for gifts and retainers.

The man will, of course, become Richard III. My thanks to Audrey Anderson of St. Paul, MN, a member of the Richard III Society and very expert on Richard. She examined this section in manuscript and made helpful suggestions to improve its accuracy. My most heavily drawn upon source of information for this section was Paul Murray Kendall's *Richard III*.

xxxii   During the agricultural year's most busy times, plowing or harvesting, a lord could, if necessary, call on his villeins for extra work days (in addition to the time they ordinarily spent working for him). In the case of harvest days, these extra work days were called "bid-reaps," and because they were ostensibly voluntary he would give the workers a "reprisal" of food and/or ale.

xxxiii   The notion that a man would simply barge in and take possession of property to which he had a weak claim is not my own. See H. S. Bennett's *The Pastons and Their England* (p. 63) for an account of how Margaret Paston had a house in which she was living virtually torn down about her ears on the orders of Lord Molyenes because of a dispute over ownership of the land the house stood on. Because the King was so busy defending (or attacking the stranger on) his throne, he had little time for administrative problems, and local strong men grew up under a kind of bastardized feudalism that allowed them to get away with almost anything they dared to try. Poor Lady Bertille's fate is taken from an actual incident described in Eileen Power's *Medieval English Nunneries*.

xxxiv   The Chamberlain was in charge of everything domestic but food, and between the Saturday night foot-washing and all the dirty laundry, she probably did not have a delicate stomach.

xxxv   *Aqua Vitae* is "water of life" in Latin. The Irish phrase for water of Life is *uisge-beatha*, and from that we get our word for it: whiskey. To re-distill whiskey, even with rosemary, must have produced an exceptionally powerful liquor. Elizabeth, Queen of Hungary, did recommend that it be used externally as well as internally. She claimed that she washed often with the stuff, and it not only cured her gout and lameness at the age of seventy, but so restored her beauty that the King of Poland came to court her! (*History of Inventions*, Vol. II by William Johnston.)

xxxvi   The long strip of colored cloth worn around a priest's neck (the "stole") symbolized Christ's cross and was an emblem of authority. Purple is for penitence. The descriptions of the Sacraments are from the *Roman Ritual*, a how-to book for priests. (Unfortunately the copy I used is an early 20th century one, whose instructions could not date earlier than the Council of Trent (1545-1563) at which much of the Catholic Church's ritual was standardized.)

xxxvii   Fifteenth century slang meaning that for all he has a glib tongue, one day he'll be executed as a felon and his corpse left hanging for crows to feast on. (Crows attack the eyes first and with relish, and my gruesome imagination is sure they are the pudding; but it should be noted that "puddings" was fifteenth century slang for human innards.)

xxxviii   It was important to Margaret that Deer Abbey date at least from the time of Edward the Confessor, as only then could it claim the special status of a Royal Abbey, which meant its direct overlord was the King, not the local Bishop. A bishop would have far more time to devote to interfering with the selection of an abbess, for example, than the King. (It should be noted that in 1107 Henry I insisted the nuns at Shaftesbury confirm his appointment of Cecilia, a daughter of Robert Fitz-Hamon, as abbess. Kings frequently interfered at the royal abbey of Shaftesbury, but

Shaftesbury was the largest, richest and most powerful in England. Its abbesses in the thirteenth century ranked as barons.) In the case of a royal abbey, the King was supposed only to license an election and confirm its result.

xxxix   A survey of Shaftesbury Abbey holdings completed in 1505 complained that all the records had been found "very confusedly in divers chests and boxes ..." (*Shaftesbury and Its Abbey*, Laura Lydenham)

xl   In 1967 I was privileged to witness bell-ringers in a Leicester, England church tower set up for and ring changes. In order that the bell begin her ring in full swing, she is "stood on her head," by ringing harder and harder, and giving a short little tug as the bell reaches the top of her swing, until she turns completely upside down and is skillfully brought to a halt. One can tell when she is nearly ready to be halted because the sound of her note changes from "ding - dong," to a peculiar "dingering - dongering."

xli   Fifteenth century slang which probably needs no translating. But a priest pointed out to me that since intent means everything in the Catholic church, there was no desecration unless Fitzralph and his men knew what they were doing would desecrate the church. I thought I'd share that bit of esoterica with you.

xlii   "Into Thy hands, O Lord, I commend his spirit." A Christian's dying act was supposed to be to put his soul into the custody of Jesus. Here Margaret, not sure Father Hugh is dead (precisely when a soul leaves a body is an ancient question), or whether he had a chance to repeat the formula, is doing it for him.

xliii   A wake merely meant an opportunity to stay up long past bedtime. The majority of people in the middle ages went to bed when it got dark and arose when it got light. Eves of holy days (holidays = no work) were frequently marked by wakes because no one had to get up at daybreak the next morning.

xliv   There is a miracle play called "The Death of Pilate" in which the body of Pontius Pilate is dragged from place to place because no one wants anything to do with him, even dead. The "very earth" tosses the unfortunate actor playing the role out of his grave every time an attempt is made to bury him.

xlv   The letter to the Duke is from an actual letter of petition to Richard of Gloucester quoted in *Richard III* by Kendall. The other letters contain period phrasing.

xlvi   It was believed that the souls of the just were escorted by angels to a *refrigerarium* called Abraham's Bosom from which they could watch the tortures of the damned while they awaited the general resurrection at the end of time. The concept is a very early one (third century) and comes from the story of Dives and Lazarus in the Gospels (Mark 16:19). Only holy innocents (baptized infants) and martyrs went directly to what we think of as heaven.

xlvii   Liam dogs hunt by scent — they are the ancestors of the bloodhound. They hunted on leashes (liam meant leash), and were very fierce. Umbles meant entrails (often specifically the heart, lungs and liver). Umble pie, anyone?

xlviii   Improvements in the manufacture of gunpowder occurred in the fifteenth century, and until improvements in the manufacture of cannon barrels caught up, there were a number of serious accidents.

xlix   Guigo de Chaulhaco, known as Guy de Chauliac, was a fourteenth century physician and surgeon (d. 1368) who rediscovered how to set bones. (The ancient Celts knew how.) He was very famous, and physician to Popes Clement IV, Innocent VI and Urban V. He did a lot of writing and his works were translated and distributed all over Europe. There are still a number of fifteenth century English manuscripts in existence. De Chauliac apparently was the one who discovered the value of suspending broken limbs while they healed.

l   The affected lisp was considered a way to make a man's voice more attractive to women. Chaucer's monk affected a lisp, and he had "children sitting by other men's fires."

li   Richard Duke of Gloucester became famous all over England for his "indifferent" (unbiased) sense of justice and was frequently asked to arbitrate in disputes. Queen Elizabeth (Elizabeth Woodville, Edward IV's wife) once sent all the way to Ireland to kill a man and his sons when she discovered the man had told her husband in private conversation that he (the King) would have done better to have made a foreign marriage, for reasons of state. She "borrowed" the royal seal to do it.

lii   The Gospel side is on the right, the Epistle side is on the left of the altar, from the point of view of the congregation. So named from where the priest stands to read these two portions of the Mass.

liii   An intricate play on words is found here: We are clay, made by God who is therefore our Potter. A Potter's Field is a cemetery for paupers —

it was widely understood in the middle ages (see the play "Everyman" for example) that our worldly goods were only loaned to us, that we were buried essentially penniless. Christians were redeemed ("bought") by Christ's death. This kind of layered intricacy is very medieval, according to Father Robert B. Wellisch, of the College of St. Thomas, who translated the prayers from the Roman Pontifical (the bishop's how-to book of ceremony). Again, unfortunately, a post-Trent copy.

liv   Titivillus was a devil whose task was to collect the dropped phrases and stepped-on words of monks, priests and nuns. If he did not collect three bags full a day, Satan beat him. His story was told to make those who repeated certain prayers with stultifying frequency give each word and phrase its due space and time, a hard task if the prayers were learned by rote.

lv   Saint Hugh of Lincoln (ca, 1135-1200) was often accompanied by a swan which loved him dearly, according to the *Life of St. Hugh* by Adam of Eynsham.

lvi   Chaplain here is a special office performed in turn by all the nuns, a new one coming on duty weekly. She carried Margaret's crozier in processions and held it while Margaret read the lessons on formal occasions, and was her travelling companion. She also served as witness to Margaret's good behavior in case of scandal. Chaucer's prioress has a nun with her serving as chaplain.

lvii   "Over the defect of her birth." Bastards lacked many of the rights of legitimate children; however, it was often possible to have at least some of these rights restored on application (and payment) to the right bishop.

lviii   There are a number of saints named Margaret, but the most popular in the late Middle Ages was a virgin martyr whose feast day is July 20. She was fictitious, a romantic legend purporting to be of the time of Diocletian, daughter of a pagan priest. She suffered many tortures for her faith, then asked God to show her the devil in a form she could understand. A dragon appeared in her cell and ate her — but she was so holy the dragon died and she emerged unharmed. Even medieval theologians doubted this tale, on the peculiar medieval-logic grounds that the devil, being a spirit, cannot die.

lix   All descriptions concerning the making of the bell are from a translation of *On Divers Arts* by Theophilus.

lx   A woman or minor child left heir to property of significance came under the protection of the King, who would assign the duties of looking out for the property to someone he owed a favor to. It was expected this person would line his pockets to the best of his ability; recognition of this fact extended so far as to disallow, by law, the receipt of any other fees or reimbursements for his efforts.

lxi   Pronounced in Church Latin BAY-nay; pronounced by locals "bean". Supposed to be a free-will favor, it survives to this day in such terms as quilting bee.

lxii   Rose hip tea has a lot of vitamin C in it, and thus has a distinct citrus flavor. Pregnant women were notorious for craving oranges, and were traditionally allowed one per pregnancy — see The Paston Letters.

lxiii   Blacksmiths were objects of awe and suspicion — fire was a feature of hell, and a person who dealt fearlessly and unburned with red-hot metal was possibly in league with the devil. Iron has many ancient superstitions attached to it; you may still buy horseshoe-nail rings in gift shops.

lxiv   Use of a sheet of brass to mark a resting place or memorialize a person dates to the thirteenth century. Until the sixteenth century, brass was imported into England, and the purchase of a slab large enough to cover a grave must have been a considerable expense. Some were turned over and reused. Of the estimated 100,000 brasses in England, only 7,500 exist today. Most were melted down; some remain in place; one was cut into a weathercock, one was made into a sundial, and one was found serving at the back of a fireplace.

lxv   A certain Sister Elizabeth saw-a man standing on the stairs and, on approach, recognized him as the devil — and she boxed his ears for having vexed her all that day!

lxvi   Through my fault, through my fault, through my most grievous fault." An acknowledgment of sinfulness from the Prayers at the Foot of the Altar said with humble breast-beating by the priest at the beginning of the old Latin Mass.

lxvii   The words spoken at the Consecration of the Mass, which turned bread and wine into the Body and Blood of Christ, had to be said absolutely correctly. A man with a speech defect could not become a priest — nor could a man without hands, as the elements had to be held a certain way.

lxviii   Adapted from one of a collection of moral tales for preachers by Etienne de Bourbon, an early friar who joined the Dominican order in about 1223. Found in *Life in the Middle Ages*, a wonderful book.

lxix   The story of this miracle is found in the Lanercost Chronicle which dates from 1307, but is based on even older material. I found the story itself in my copy of *Life in the Middle Ages*, but the commentary elsewhere — I forget where.

lxx   All the accusations — and more — made against Lady Josiana in the bishop's letter were made against a real abbess, Margaret Wavere, in 1442. Margaret's defense — and lack of compurgesses — was the same as Josiana's, but she kept her post.

lxxi   A story from *Revelation to a Monk of Eynsham*, first printed in English in 1483. It was written in Latin by Adam, twelfth century subprior of Eynsham (near Oxford), the same man who wrote from first-hand knowledge the charming *Life of St. Hugh*. The Revelation is a Dante-like story of a vision of hell.

lxxii   A common practice. Such a man could persuade many to donate goods or money, or leave things to the abbey in their wills. Eileen Power cites the records of a little Augustinian nunnery in Norfolk, which rebuilt its church: 20 pounds from John Lawson, 20 marks from Jon Watson "for his soul," 20 marks from Stevyn York, 21 marks from the Guild of the Trinity; and an individual paid for the stalls of the reredos and another offered 26 marks for two "antiphoneres" in the "queer" (choir). Lady Eleanor is not nearly so much of a builder as Joan Wiggenhall, who spent her entire rule building and rebuilding, beginning with a barn, then roofing the chancel, rebuilding her private chamber, making a malthouse with a dovecote, repairing the bakehouse, re-roofing the steeple with lead and slating the cloister roof, then undertaking on her greatest work, as noted above, building a new church. Joan died in 1451. The abbey was suppressed, its buildings unroofed for their lead and left to ruin less than a century later.

lxxiii   From *The English Physician*, a 1653 collection of even-then-old folk remedies by Thomas Culpeper. A modern doctor told me the ointment would work as described.

lxxiv   Based on an actual incident — only it was to the child's father that the abbess sent the girl, and he was as indignant about her ignorance as her thinness and rags. Various bishops put various restrictions on nunneries wishing to take in students. One abbey at the time of the suppression was educating twenty-six children!

lxxv   Master Einar Lutemaker suggests that the charcoal of the stick sets up a chemical reaction that removes impurities from the molten bronze.

lxxvi   "Into Thy hands ... " The last words of any Christian were supposed to be the same as Christ's: "Into Thy hands (I commend my spirit"). Here there is a play on words, and one assumes Lady Margaret was found with a smile on her lips. She also died ignorant of the bad news Freemantle was bringing: Richard III had gone down to defeat and death at Bosworth Field; England was left in the hands of the infamous Henry VII.

lxxvii   Invented by myself.

Author's Commentary

This book is put together from four "chapbooks" I wrote back in the 1980s as a study for a character I'd invented: Margaret of Shaftesbury, Abbess. She lived from 1400 to 1485, mostly in a small nunnery in the foothills of the Cotswolds called the Abbey of the White Stag (*Abatia Cervi Albi*, after the vision of St. Eustace). AKA Deer Abbey.

Its Mass Priest is "a small brown fellow with kind, anxious eyes, who means well" named Father Hugh of Paddington. I wrote about one a year, and now Ellen and I have drawn the chapbooks together to make a novel of a little over two hundred pages, if you include the endnotes.

The chapbooks were thoroughly researched but lightly written, self-published, and earned me a Laurel in the Society for Creative Anachronism. I've always been fond of the story that they tell, but didn't really notice until now, editing them as one piece of writing, how my writing improved as they went along. The last one is really rather fine.

Mary Kuhfeld